THE COLTONS:
COMANCHE BLOOD

*Discover a proud, passionate clan
of men and women who will risk everything
for love, family and honor.*

Jesse Colton:
As a special government agent, danger
comes with the job. But protecting breathtaking
Samantha Cosgrove—and his heart—could prove
to be his toughest assignment ever.

Samantha Cosgrove:
The sweet, idealistic campaign staffer has stumbled
upon a troubling secret. Only Jesse Colton can help
her discover the truth—and unlock the passions
hidden inside her.

Gloria Whitebear:
Will the secret past of the Oklahoma Coltons'
matriarch come back to haunt her grandchildren?

Sky Colton:
Jesse's hardworking younger sister is fast becoming
famous for her Native American jewelry. But life
has a very different design in store for this
independent woman.

Dear Reader,

Summer is over and it's time to kick back into high gear. Just be sure to treat yourself with a luxuriant read or two (or, hey, all six) from Silhouette Romance. Remember—work hard, play harder!

Although October is officially Breast Cancer Awareness month, we'd like to invite you to start thinking about it now. In a wonderful, uplifting story, a rancher reluctantly agrees to model for a charity calendar to earn money for cancer research. At the back of that book, we've also included a guide for self-exams. Don't miss Cara Colter's must-read *9 Out of 10 Women Can't Be Wrong* (#1615).

Indulge yourself with megapopular author Karen Rose Smith and her CROWN AND GLORY series installment, *Searching for Her Prince* (#1612). A missing heir puts love on the line when he hides his identity from the woman assigned to track him down. The royal, brooding hero in Sandra Paul's stormy *Caught by Surprise* (#1614), the latest in the A TALE OF THE SEA adventure, also has secrets—and intends to make his beautiful captor pay…by making her his wife!

Jesse Colton is a special agent forced to play pretend boyfriend to uncover dangerous truths in the fourth of THE COLTONS: COMANCHE BLOOD spinoff, *The Raven's Assignment* (#1613), by bestselling author Kasey Michaels. And in Cathie Linz's MEN OF HONOR title, *Married to a Marine* (#1616), combat-hardened Justice Wilder had shut himself away from the world—until his ex-wife's younger sister comes knocking.… Finally, in Laurey Bright's tender and true *Life with Riley* (#1617), free-spirited Riley Morrisset may not be the perfect society wife, but she's exactly what her stiff-collared boss needs!

Happy reading—and please keep in touch.

Mary-Theresa Hussey

Mary-Theresa Hussey
Senior Editor

Please address questions and book requests to:
Silhouette Reader Service
U.S.: 3010 Walden Ave., P.O. Box 1325, Buffalo, NY 14269
Canadian: P.O. Box 609, Fort Erie, Ont. L2A 5X3

The Raven's Assignment

KASEY MICHAELS

SILHOUETTE *Romance*®

Published by Silhouette Books

America's Publisher of Contemporary Romance

Special thanks and acknowledgment are given
to Kasey Michaels for her contribution
to THE COLTONS series.

To Julie Barrett, who has the patience of a saint.

 SILHOUETTE BOOKS

ISBN 0-373-19613-X

THE RAVEN'S ASSIGNMENT

Books by Kasey Michaels

Silhouette Romance

Maggie's Miscellany #331
Compliments of the Groom #542
Popcorn and Kisses #572
To Marry at Christmas #616
His Chariot Awaits #701
Romeo in the Rain #743
Lion on the Prowl #808
Sydney's Folly #834
Prenuptial Agreement #898
Uncle Daddy #916
Marriage in a Suitcase #949
Timely Matrimony #1030
The Dad Next Door #1108
Carried Away #1438
   "Logan Assents"
*Marrying Maddy #1469
*Jessie's Expecting #1475
*Raffling Ryan #1481
Bachelor on the Prowl #1552
The Raven's Assignment #1613

*The Chandlers Request

American Romance

His Innocent Temptress #869
The McCallum Quintuplets #909
   "Great Expectations"

Silhouette Yours Truly

Husbands Don't Grow on Trees

Harlequin Love & Laughter

Five's a Crowd

Silhouette Books

Baby Fever

36 Hours
Strange Bedfellows

The Fortunes of Texas
The Sheik's Secret Son

The Coltons
Beloved Wolf
The Hopechest Bride

KASEY MICHAELS

is the *New York Times* and *USA TODAY* bestselling author of more than sixty books. She has won the Romance Writers of America RITA® Award and the *Romantic Times* Career Achievement Award for her historical romances set in the Regency era, and also writes contemporary romances for Silhouette and Harlequin Books.

THE COLTONS: COMANCHE BLOOD

George WhiteBear

?
m Theodore Colton (d) m Gloria WhiteBear

Kay Barkley (d)
See "The Coltons"

Thomas Colton m Alice Callahan

Sally SharpStone (d) m Trevor Colton (d)

(2) Bram m Jenna Elliot

    Ashe

(1) Jared m Kerry WindWalker

    Logan

    Peggy

(3) Willow m Tyler Chadwick

(7) Grey

(5) Billy

(4) Jesse m Samantha Cosgrove

(6) Sky

Shane

Seth

(1) WHITE DOVE'S PROMISE
by Stella Bagwell SE #1478 On sale 7/02

(2) THE COYOTE'S CRY
by Jackie Merritt SE #1484 On sale 8/02

(3) WILLOW IN BLOOM
by Victoria Pade SE #1490 On sale 9/02

(4) THE RAVEN'S ASSIGNMENT
by Kasey Michaels SR #1613 On sale 9/02

(5) A COLTON FAMILY CHRISTMAS
by various authors On sale 10/02

(6) SKY FULL OF PROMISE
by Teresa Southwick SR #1624 On sale 11/02

(7) THE WOLF'S SURRENDER
by Sandra Steffen SR #1630 On sale 12/02

LEGEND:
m Married
d Deceased
   Twins

Chapter One

*P*OTUS *is on the move.*

"Copy that."

"Copy what, Sean? It's a little late for activity from the residence, isn't it?" Jesse Colton asked, looking up from the page he'd been reading as he walked through the West Wing toward the doors and what was left of his evening.

"Nothing, Jesse," Sean said, no longer talking into his shirt collar. "POTUS is on the move. It's nearly midnight, so he's on the way to the main kitchen, probably. FLOTUS keeps stashing the residence fridge with apples and pears. POTUS wants coconut-cream pie."

"I wonder what the American Heart Association would have to say about President's sweet tooth," Jesse said, perching on a corner of Sean's desk just inside the main vestibule. As jobs went, Sean's was pretty cushy—but guarding the West Wing was also pretty boring. "And the loyal opposition would probably start demanding monthly cholesterol checks."

"Yes, but with us all sworn to fall on our swords rather than play tattletale, I guess POTUS is safe, both from the AHA and FLOTUS."

Jesse looked at the small, boxy screen on Sean's desk, a constantly updated listing showing the location of the first family. Sure enough, POTUS, better known as President Jackson Coates, now showed in the main kitchen, with FLOTUS still in the second-floor residence, probably sound asleep. "POTUS. President of the United States. FLOTUS, first lady of the etcetera, etcetera. The acronyms ought to sound more presidential, don't you think?"

"I'll mention it at tomorrow's meeting of the Proper Presidential Acronym Committee—that would be P-PAC, of course," Sean said, shaking his head. Sean was the perfect Secret Service agent; his hair was neatly clipped, his suit neatly pressed, and his smile neatly neutral. "What do you have there, Jesse?"

Jesse looked down at the now-closed manila folder. "This? Personal stuff. Don't worry, I'm not planning to remove state secrets on your watch, and sell them to the tabloids. I mean, how much could they pay for a headline like POTUS Caught in Coconut-Cream Orgy."

"That's a relief. So, what do you have there?"

Jesse grinned. "That's it, Sean, trust nobody."

"No, seriously. You were frowning. Frowning over personal stuff is never a good thing."

Jesse opened the folder and looked at the single sheet

inside. "My family seems to have inherited a house in Georgetown."

"And this is bad news? Georgetown? Cushy address. Oh, wait a minute. Does it come with fifty years of back taxes they all want you to pay because you're getting rich here at the White House, feeding from the public trough?"

"Not quite, no," Jesse said, knowing that if Sean knew the whole truth, he'd probably fall off his chair. "The place has been rented out for about sixty years now. I'm just trying to figure out a way to explain to the Senate Ethics Committee how I, a lowly public servant, came to be part owner of the Chekagovian embassy."

"You're kidding," Sean said, grabbing for the folder, which Jesse quickly raised beyond his reach. "Is that legal? I mean, for a member of the president's staff to own part of a foreign consulate?"

"I probably own a third of the garage, Sean. There's a bunch of us who each own a small chunk of the place. The whole Colton tribe, as we call ourselves when we're being facetious, inherited it. But I'll admit, it is dicey. I mean, if we have a slow news week, who knows what could happen if this gets out. So I guess I have to tell…somebody."

"Chief of staff?"

Jesse blew out a quick breath. "Might as well start at the top." He slid the folder back into his briefcase and stood up. "Luckily, he went home at a decent hour, so it will have to wait. Besides, I need to do a little more digging into the deed, all that legal stuff, to be sure of my facts. See you tomorrow, Sean."

"See you, Mr. Moneybags, Mr. I-Own-Part-of-Georgetown," Sean called after him, then said, "Hey, wait! I forgot something."

"You never forget anything, Sean," Jesse said, slowly walking back to the desk. "You just want to pump me for more information."

"Not me. The more you know the less you want to know, that's my byword. No, seriously," he said, rooting through some messages on his desk. "This came in late, after your secretary left. Now where in hell—ah, got it."

He handed Jesse a "while you were out" memo.

Jesse frowned at the unfamiliar name as he read the memo. "Urgent? You did see that part of the message, right, Sean? The *urgent* part?"

"Hey, everything's urgent around here. The message arrived via the main switchboard, after being routed to the OEOB first, and then a couple of other places, which is probably how I ended up with it."

"The Old Executive Office Building? I haven't worked there in months."

"Well, guess not everyone knows you've been bumped up to a big-deal office in the West Wing. You should have taken an ad. Most do."

"Funny, Sean," Jesse said, heading out once more, this time frowning over the pink memo. "Samantha Cosgrove. Urgent. Now, who the hell is Samantha Cosgrove?"

Samantha Cosgrove, all the long blond hair and petitely formed five feet four inches of her, sat behind her desk, staring daggers at her telephone.

She hadn't gone on her coffee break with Bettyann. She had turned down lunch with Rita.

She hadn't left her desk all day. She was starving, and her stomach had begun to growl, she was nervous, and she was beginning to get angry.

Okay, so she'd been angry at one o'clock. It was now quarter to five. Now she was incensed.

Bettyann, the staff secretary, stuck her head inside the small office. "I'm heading out now, Samantha. Dinner at the golden arches? My treat."

"No thanks, Bettyann," Samantha said, pretending an interest in a pile of campaign literature that was about as exciting as the Weather Channel on a calm, clear day across America.

That's what the latest slogan was all about: a calm, clear-minded, new day across America. Vote for Senator Mark Phillips for President. *Bor-ring*. Surely somebody, somewhere, could come up with something better than that?

"You sure, Sam? You haven't eaten anything all day, except for that cupcake you stole from Rita. Her only satisfaction is that it had been sitting on her desk for two days, and had to be very, very stale."

"It was," Samantha said, sighing. "Okay, I'm going home. The world will keep on turning without me if I go home. But no thanks to the golden arches, Bettyann. I can hear leftover stuffed peppers calling my name."

"Right. See you here tomorrow."

"See me here, will she?" Samantha grumbled about a half hour later, grimacing as she shoved work into her briefcase. "Why not. Where else would I be?"

She grabbed her light, full-length burgundy raincoat

and followed a few other stragglers into the elevator once she'd looked through the outgoing mail, first checking to be sure nobody saw her.

Once outside, Samantha turned right and headed toward the White House on foot.

She had seen photographs of Jesse Colton, so she knew what he looked like: about six feet tall, short black hair, dark eyes. Sort of mysterious-looking, even primal.

"Okay, so he's a hunk," Samantha muttered to herself as she pulled up her hood, because it had begun to drizzle. Even in the rain, she loved living in Washington, D.C.

She'd been back in town for two years, because it took at least two years for a presidential candidate like Senator Mark Phillips to float test balloons to see if anyone would vote for him, pretend for months that he wasn't interested in running, announce the setting up of an informal Phillips for President Committee, talk to the money people, promise everybody everything, and then finally announce his formal candidacy.

Now, with the primaries beginning soon in New Hampshire, the Committee to Elect Mark Phillips had gone into full swing, had gone public, and Samantha was working hard.

She just needed to know if she was working hard for the right man.

Jesse Colton might work in the West Wing now, as she'd been informed, but she already knew he still had to walk to his old parking space, in a parking garage some distance away. It was easier to get into the West

Wing than it was to get a better parking place near the White House.

He drove a black sedan, nondescript, yet somehow classy. He arrived at the parking garage by seven o'clock in the morning, six days a week, and could leave again anywhere between five o'clock and midnight.

She knew, because she'd watched him for five long, worrisome days before making the call yesterday. The call that hadn't been returned today.

"Not stalking, Samantha, watching," she assured herself tightly as she quickly joined some other people as if she belonged with them, and then stepped into the parking garage, out of the drizzle that was rapidly turning into a downpour. "There's a difference."

The difference, she decided two hours later, was that stalkers probably planned better. Maybe even brought a peanut butter and jelly sandwich and a thermos of piping-hot coffee with them.

She'd finally given in and jogged to a small local restaurant to grab a take-out hot dog and a soda, along with a bag of potato chips, then jogged all the way back to breathe a sigh of relief when she saw the black sedan still in its assigned parking spot.

It was nine o'clock and she had begun fantasizing about peanut butter and jelly sandwiches again, when she finally saw him.

She thought it was him. She could be delirious from lack of food, but she was ninety-nine percent sure the man walking toward her was Jesse Colton.

When he clicked something on his key chain and the black sedan's lights went on, she was sure.

Stepping out from behind her second home—the concrete pillar—she said, "Jesse Colton? If I could have a minute of your time, please?"

He kept walking. "Call my office."

"I did."

"Did you leave a message?"

"I did. For you to call me. You didn't."

"Now there's a clue," he said, opening the rear door of the sedan and throwing his briefcase inside. "It's late. If you want an interview, go through the press secretary's office."

"I don't want an interview," she said, walking toward him. "I'm not a reporter."

"Darn. And I'll bet you're not this generation's Deep Throat, either, ready to tell me deep dark secrets, or Mr. White, who was going to let me know that Mr. Green did it, in the library, with the rope. I don't get any luck."

He had opened his car door and slid inside, but before he could close the door again, Samantha was there, her body between the door and the car.

"Are you always an ass?" she asked him, shaking her head so that her hood slipped off. She reached beneath her collar and freed her long blond hair, let some of the thick curls spill onto her shoulders.

She wasn't dumb. She was blond, fairly pretty, and had fabulous legs. She had yet to meet a single man in D.C. who had found her unattractive.

"Am I being propositioned?" Jesse asked, and his smile was a little too amused for Samantha's comfort.

"No!" she said, backing up a pace. Which was a bad move, but she realized that too late.

"Pity," he said, then reached out and closed the door. But then he rolled down the window. "You're Samantha Cosgrove, right?"

She bent down, looked in the window. "You knew that?"

"Oh yeah, I knew that. Blond, pretty and tenacious as a bulldog. I had you checked out."

"Why?"

"Because you want to talk to me. Do you have any idea how many people want to talk to me, Samantha Cosgrove, now that I'm in the West Wing?"

"Oh, aren't we popular. I'm so impressed."

"I'll bet you are. I know I am," he said, flashing her that whiter-than-white smile again.

She wanted to bang him over the head with her briefcase. Instead, she turned her back and began walking away.

"Hungry?" he asked, backing up the sedan so that he was beside her once more.

"Only if I could find a way to make your entrails appetizing," she said, and kept walking.

He kept backing up. "Ah, don't go away mad, Samantha. I was going to call you."

"When? Christmas?"

"No, I go home to Oklahoma for Christmas. Tomorrow. I was going to call you tomorrow. First I had to check you out."

"Did I pass?" she asked, interested, but she kept walking. The man set her teeth on edge.

"Well, let's see what I've got. Daughter of megarich parents residing in Connecticut after living here for decades. One brother, younger, still in college. Freshman,

I believe. One sister, older, a literary agent. Juliet, right? Mommy does charity work and belongs to all the right social groups. Daddy's a lawyer, and personal friends with and a large contributor to the presidential primary campaign for Senator Mark Phillips, who is personally endorsed by my boss, the current president. Graduated with honors, double major, in both journalism and political science. Very nice, Samantha. *Cum laude.* Even nicer. Senior staffer on Phillips's committee. Hardworking, clean-living, good cook, lousy dancer—''

"I am not a lousy dancer! I'm a very *good* dancer," Samantha protested hotly, stopping so that she could turn, glare at him.

"And here I thought you weren't listening. Okay, good dancer, although that wasn't in my report. So, you want to go get something to eat, and then prove to me that you're really a good dancer?"

"I wouldn't dance with you for all the tea in—"

"You did say *urgent,*" he interrupted.

"Are you always this arrogant?"

"No, it comes with the White House credentials. Honest. You can look at the job description. It's right there—once cleared to work in the West Wing and given a blue badge, arrogance is mandatory. Red badge? Orange badge? I spit on red and orange badges."

"You're insane," Samantha said, but then she laughed. She couldn't help herself. "Really. Insane."

"But I'm buying. How about a New York strip, since you look ready to bite something. Baked potato dripping in sour cream. A good bottle of white zinfandel? You look like a white-zinfandel drinker to me.''

"I like merlot.''

"So much for my source. I'll have to order her head chopped off in the morning. So, are you getting in, or are you just going to take the Metro home and eat those leftover filled peppers?''

"How did you—oh my God. It's true. You people know *everything*. You had someone in my house? Going through my refrigerator?''

"Nothing that illegal. But Brenda—she's my secretary—did happen to stop in at Senator Phillips's election headquarters late this afternoon. She told me someone named Bettyann would have given out your shoe size if anyone asked. Brenda also told me that you're blond and a looker. She was right. Now, come on. Get in.''

Samantha threw up her hands. "Why not. I deserve a free steak after you invaded my privacy that way. You *are* buying, you know.''

"I wouldn't have it any other way,'' he said once she was in the passenger seat, her briefcase on the floor.

"Neither would I,'' she said, arranging her oversize raincoat across her legs. He didn't deserve to see her legs. "And then we'll talk?''

"And then we'll talk. Promise,'' he said, slipping the car into Drive and heading out of the parking deck. "But first we eat. I don't know about you, but I'm starving.''

"I can relate,'' Samantha said, hoping her stomach wouldn't growl before she could feed it.

* * *

Finding an empty table in any half-decent restaurant close to the White House was darn near impossible, anytime day or night, but as they approached one of the best ones, Samantha told him to pull up out front at the valet service area.

"Much as I'd like to tell you I'm even smarter than my personnel file says I am, I didn't know you were going to be lying in wait for me in the parking lot, or that you'd agree to come to dinner with me. That said, I don't have reservations."

"That's all right. Just pull over."

He did, and the valet opened the passenger-side door. Samantha accepted the hand she was offered, and said, "Good evening, Anthony. It's good to see you again."

"And it's wonderful to see you again, Ms. Cosgrove," Anthony the valet said, guiding her under the canopy and out of the rain.

"I guess I'm just supposed to schlep it on my own," Jesse grumbled to himself as Anthony and his large black golf umbrella didn't move from the canopy again.

He got out, tossed his keys to Anthony, and found himself following Samantha inside the dimly lit foyer of the restaurant known for its old boys' club decor and aged steaks.

She was already standing in front of the podium, with an Anthony look-alike holding her raincoat over his arm, and speaking fluent Italian with the maître d'.

A few more Italian phrases, some sharp snapping of the fingers by the maître d', and they were being escorted past the line of diners waiting to be seated and to a prime table. Jesse was pretty sure he recognized a representative from Pennsylvania in the line, as well as a second assistant undersecretary of state.

"How'd you do that?" he asked once they were seated.

"So much for your thorough research. I was raised in the District, remember, before Dad decided to relocate in Connecticut. I've known Anthony and his family for years, since my father and mother first began coming here," she told him as she spread her napkin in her lap.

Then she leaned forward and said with an unholy grin on her lovely, patrician face, "You see, Mr. Colton? Badges? I don't need no steenkin' badges."

If he were less a man of the world, Jesse would have believed he fell in love with Samantha Cosgrove the moment the words were out of her mouth.

Instead, he threw back his head and laughed, and banished any other thoughts as unprofessional. And definitely personally dangerous.

They were handed oversize menus, leather-clad, and Jesse watched as Samantha frowned over hers.

She was so blond. So sleek. So High Society.

And he was the part Comanche nobody from Black Arrow, Oklahoma.

Man. Who would have thunk it.

"I think I want two of everything," she said at last, smiling at him overtop the menu. "Is that all right?"

"That depends. How good are you at washing dishes?"

"Ah, the woefully underpaid public servant," Samantha said, closing the menu and placing it beside her cutlery so that she could fold her hands on the tabletop. "Do you like it?"

"Being a public servant, or being underpaid?" he asked, closing his own menu.

"No, seriously, do you like it? I mean, I get chills, just thinking about the West Wing. The Oval Office. All that power, all in one place."

"And the doughnuts ain't bad," Jesse said, grinning.

She sat back. "All right, so I'm not immune to the idea that you work in the West Wing. It's heady. How did you get there, anyway?"

"Hard work, determination, knowing the right people—all that good stuff."

"Will you please be serious. I mean, I know you started in the Secret Service."

"Not much of a secret, is it?" he commented, trying to look upset. "And then I moved on to the NSA—National Security Agency."

"Yes, and from there to the West Wing. One of the president's trusted advisers. I don't remember reading that you stopped a bullet for him, or anything like that."

"No, nothing that dramatic. Let's just say I'm ambitious, and that, yes, I did know the right people, and that I was in the right place at the right time. When the president's second term is over, and your guy's in the Oval Office, I'll head back to the NSA. I'm only on loan, you know. That was the deal."

"You won't want to be part of Phillips's staff?"

"I won't be asked. Same party, Samantha, but each man comes in with his own people. And, frankly, I think I'll be glad. The NSA is where I really want to be. I'm not all that political. I'd rather think I'm serving my country, not just the current administration. Since the president agreed, and really wants more of an outsider's opinion on national security, we're fine. This was, hell, this was an ego thing as much as anything else. But enough about me. Why do you want to be part of Phillips's staff?''

The waiter approached, and they both gave their orders, then were silent as the wine—compliments of the owner—was opened and poured.

''Nice touch, even if I am going to have to pay for it. We're not allowed to accept gifts, you know. Still, I could get used to this,'' Jesse said, sipping the wine. ''So, Samantha, are you going to tell me? Why do you want to be part of Phillips's staff?''

''Because he's right for America,'' Samantha said, and then she grimaced. ''Okay, okay, the truth. Not that he isn't right for America. He's a wonderful man. But to get the chance to walk into the West Wing? Stand inside the Oval Office? Be even a small piece of the power behind the man in that office? You've admitted it, so I can say it. Who wouldn't want that?''

''True, true. Fifteen-hour days, constant emergencies, news leaks, congressmen who need their hands held. It's great.''

''You're just saying that. I don't think you'd ever be anywhere you didn't want to be.''

Jesse didn't answer her. He just lifted his glass in salute and took another sip of wine as the waiter placed large bowls of salad in front of them.

Oh, he liked this woman. He really, really liked her.

And she was correct. He was right where he wanted to be. Across the table from a very interesting woman.

By the time they'd finished their steaks, Jesse was feeling pretty mellow.

Mellow enough to ask a question he probably shouldn't have asked.

"Have you ever been to the Chekagovian embassy?" he asked, because it seemed as if she'd been everywhere else in the District, and most parts of Virginia. She knew everybody, probably through her parents or Senator Phillips, and had been invited to all the right parties.

Samantha sat back and rolled her eyes. "Oh, the Chekagovian embassy! Isn't it beautiful?"

"I don't know. I've never seen it." That much was true. He'd only gotten the fax from the local law firm yesterday, and was still trying to grasp the idea that he and his relatives owned the pricey mansion...and the rest of it.

"You've never seen it? Oh, you have to see it. I mean, I've never been inside, but from the outside? The grounds are magnificent, just for starters. I was there for a photo op with the senator's wife, but we didn't get to go inside. Gorgeous gardens, with flowers all over—"

"I've heard that. Gardens, with flowers in them. Very unique."

"Don't be funny," she said, then waited until their plates were cleared from the table. "And it's not just the gardens. The mansion is truly extraordinary. Federal style. Wonderful old redbrick. A million windows. Exterior wood all painted creamy white, and definitely handcrafted by experts. It's...it's a slice of American history. Really."

"And it serves as the Chekagovian embassy."

She nodded. "That's what happened to so many of the best old houses. It's the price we pay for being the center of the political world. Of course, if we weren't, who knows what would have happened to those lovely old mansions."

"They'd never have been built."

"Good point. I hadn't thought of that. Anyway, I'd love to get inside that place, just for a look around. Why did you mention it?"

Jesse drew back, knowing he'd probably already said too much. "Oh, no real reason. I'd just heard it was a...a nice place."

Her gorgeous blue eyes narrowed. "Liar."

"I beg your pardon," he said as the waiter poured coffee for them. "I never lie."

"Oh, the new millennium's George Washington. You cannot tell a lie. This city hasn't seen another one like him, until you, of course. I'm so impressed. Really."

"All right, all right," Jesse said, holding out his hands. "But only because you dragged it out of me at fork-point."

"I did not," she told him. "That was next."

Jesse laughed. He didn't know if the good food had made him feel so comfortable, or the good wine...or the great company. What he did know was that if he didn't soon tell someone what he'd learned in that fax, he was probably going to burst. Just like a little kid with good news.

"First I have to swear you to secrecy," he told her.

"Certainly," she said, then held up her right hand. "I, Samantha Cosgrove, do solemnly swear that I won't breathe a word of what Jesse Colton is about to tell me, so help me spit. There. Is that good enough?"

"Pretty good. Although I'll still have to kill you once you know everything."

"That seems only fair. You were Secret Service. Does that mean you could kill me with a rubber band or pencil sharpener?"

"We don't do those anymore. Now we use Post-it notes. I'm hell with a Post-it note."

"I'll bet you are. Now, come on, tell me. What do I want to know about the Chekagovian embassy?"

"That I own it?" he said, raising his eyebrows.

"That you…that you…oh, you fibber you. You *own* it? Well, that makes us even. I own the Washington Monument. Oh, and we rent out the Lincoln Memorial. Tax reasons, you know."

He smiled, shook his head. "I know, it's hard to believe, but I own it. Really. Well, I own some of it."

"Some of it," she repeated, spooning three sugars into her coffee.

"Hey, easy on the sugar."

"Never mind me. You'd better take yours black, because I think you've had too much wine, and you'll need to sober up before you drive home."

"You think I'm handing you a line?" he asked, tipping his head to one side as he looked at her. God, she had a wise mouth. He loved to hear her talk. He'd love more to shut her up…with his own mouth.

"If you are, I have to admit I've never heard this

particular one before tonight. So, if I promise to be good, and not laugh too hard, why don't you tell me *why* you own part of the mansion?''

''That would take until tomorrow morning,'' Jesse said, wincing. ''So we'll leave that for another time, if that's all right with you.''

''There's going to be another time?''

''If you want, yes. But it's getting late, and I've got a six-thirty meeting at the White House. So…''

''So I should tell you my reason for contacting you in the first place? For…for stalking you?''

''What a good idea,'' he said, grinning. ''You can tell me part of it, the way I told you part of mine, and then we'll go on from there. If you want to.''

''I shouldn't. You're much, much too sure of yourself, Jesse Colton.''

''It's a failing, I agree. So? Do we have a deal?''

She nodded. ''We have a deal. But not here, there are too many ears. Pay the check, and I'll tell you once you drive me home. At the curb, Colton—I'm not inviting you into my house. Agreed?''

He eased his wallet from his slacks pocket and pulled out a credit card. ''Agreed. Spoilsport.''

They left the restaurant after Samantha was kissed on both cheeks by the maître d', two interchangeable Anthonys and a plump woman who came out from the kitchen, wiping her hands on an apron as she called out, ''Bella! Sweet Bella!''

''Are you this popular in all the District restaurants? If so, I think ours could be a beautiful relationship, at least until my credit card maxes out.''

''I'll bet everyone in every gym in town knows

you," she said as he tried to open the car door for her, only to be beaten out by Anthony Number One.

When he slid in behind the wheel, he said, "Actually, they know me at most of the museums. I'm big on museums."

"I wouldn't have guessed that," she said as he pulled away from the curb. "Head toward Dupont Circle, and I'll give you directions from there."

Fifteen minutes later he pulled the sedan over to the curb in front of an old redbrick town house. "Apartment?" he asked, looking at the well-kept building.

"Mom and Dad's place, for when they come to the city. We never sold it. Juliet doesn't stay here, not that she's ever in town, but I'm the younger daughter, and part of my permission to come here to work hinged on my agreeing to stay at the old homestead. Mom's a worrywart," she told him, fishing in her purse for her key and not finding it. "Now, remember that sworn-to-secrecy stuff?"

"Hope to spit," he said, turning off the ignition, knowing the windows would fog up within minutes. But if he didn't turn off the ignition, the chances were lower that he'd be invited in for a nightcap. Hope to spit, yes. And hope springs eternal—that was Jesse's motto, or at least it was since meeting Samantha Cosgrove.

She took a deep breath, then stared through the rapidly steaming-up windshield, her fingers nervously opening and closing the snap on her purse. "I have fairly varied duties at campaign headquarters. I handle press releases sometimes, organize fund-raisers, help write some of the lesser important speeches. Even lick stamps if we're shorthanded. I do everything.''

"All right," Jesse said, and that's all he said, because he could tell that Samantha was nervous and still might change her mind about talking to him.

"In the course of my…duties," she went on after a moment, her cheeks pale in the light of a strong street-lamp across the way, "I learned a few names. More than a few names. I learned yours, for instance."

"But not my whereabouts, because you tried to reach me through the OEOB."

"I used an old directory," she said with a wave of her hand. "That doesn't matter. What matters is that you have a reputation, Jesse."

"Whatever it is, I didn't do it," he said, then winced. "Sorry. It was getting a little tense in here. I thought I'd try to lighten the mood."

"That's all right. I'm not saying this very well. This is embarrassing, because I'm usually very good with words. But you do have a reputation, Jesse. For honesty. For being a straight shooter. For being intensely loyal and definitely trustworthy."

"Now I'm embarrassed."

She shifted on the seat, turning to face him. "Last week," she began, then closed her eyes for a moment before looking at him again. "Oh, this is so hard."

"Just say it fast, Samantha," he advised her, taking her hand in his. Her fingers were icy cold, nearly bloodless. He didn't know what was wrong, but whatever it was, she wasn't only worried, she was scared.

"All right. Last week, Thursday, I think, I…I was licking stamps. I mean, not really licking stamps, but I was there late, and there was mail to go out, and since I was there and had no plans, I stayed to do it.''

Jesse's radar switched on. Mail. Mail leaving a senator's campaign office. The possibilities were endless. ''Go on,'' he urged when she stopped speaking.

''I can't. I can't do this. Senator Phillips has been so good to me. And my father? He adores the man. They were in the army together. I mean, I used to call him Uncle Mark. I still do, in private.''

''Samantha, sorry, but you can't stop here. What was in the mail?''

''Outgoing mail,'' she clarified, then sighed. ''It had to be a mistake. I mean, he wouldn't do anything wrong, I know he wouldn't.''

''What was in the mail?'' Jesse repeated, squeezing her fingers.

''Something…something that shouldn't even have been in there, in the campaign office,'' she said quietly, pulling her hand free. ''You know he chairs the Senate Ways and Means Committee, and they deal with some very sensitive material…''

''Money, Samantha. They deal with a lot of money. In Washington, money equals power, and power equals money. Now, one more time, Samantha. What was in the mail?''

''Tomorrow,'' she said quickly, one hand on the door handle. ''Come to the office tomorrow evening. Around seven. Everybody else should be gone. I…I'll show you then.''

''You didn't send it out?''

She shook her head. ''No. I couldn't. I'm sure that

information should never have been released. I
shouldn't even have *seen* it.''

"Did you also save the envelope?" Jesse asked,
thinking ahead.

"Yes. That's how I got to see the contents. The envelope wasn't sealed correctly and the glue was all
gone. I wanted to tape it shut but couldn't find any
tape—sometimes our office is a real mess—so I slipped
everything out of the envelope to put it into a new one
and I saw...I saw..." Her voice was so quiet he had
to lean over to hear her above the sound of rain pelting
the roof of the sedan. "I'll...I'll show you everything.''

She opened the car door, then turned back, grabbed
his arm. "But you can't tell anybody. Not until we
know exactly what's going on. I mean, it was the senator's mail, but that doesn't mean that he—''

"We'll talk about it tomorrow, Samantha," Jesse
said, putting his hand over hers. "It's probably nothing.''

"That's what I think. It's nothing. Just a...a mistake.
Good night.''

And then she was gone, running through the rain to
the steps of the town house. She knocked, and a few
moments later a uniformed maid opened the door, spill-
ing mellow yellow light out onto the brick sidewalk.

"Nice work if you can get it," Jesse muttered, putting the car in gear to head home to a sleepless night.

Chapter Two

At ten o'clock the next morning, Jesse passed by the well-dressed secretary who held the door open for him, and into the large, teak-paneled law office of Rand Colton, oldest son of former Senator Joseph Colton.

His relatives. Amazing. A whole, huge branch of the family Jesse and his family hadn't known existed until a few short weeks ago. The wealthy, socially and politically prominent branch of the family, about as far away from Oklahoma and Black Arrow as a person could get.

He'd seen photographs of Senator Colton, read stories of the scandal and murders and near tragedies that had nearly torn the California family apart.

He'd run several Colton names through the Internet, read the microfiche newspaper articles at the library, and had come to the conclusion that the last thing these people needed was for another problem to rear its ugly head, both privately and for public consumption.

The public had consumed plenty already, with the murder attempts on the former senator by both his business partner and his supposed wife.

That had been the double whammy, that his wife had been the victim of amnesia for ten years while her twin sister, a convicted murderer, had impersonated her, taken her place in Joe Colton's house, Joe Colton's bed.

Bizarre.

It was the stuff of tabloids, made for TV docudramas, all that sleazy stuff. Except it all had happened to good people.

But all of that was over, in the past. Problems solved, lives mended, the future bright.

Until these latest revelations that, thankfully, were still hiding under the press's radar. Until, if the information Jesse had received thus far was correct, it had been learned that his grandmother had been the legal wife of Joe Colton's father, Teddy. The *only* legal wife of Joe Colton's father.

Making Senator Joseph Colton the bastard born on the wrong side of the blanket. Oh yeah, the tabloids would gobble it up if they knew. One thing Jesse wanted to make very clear to the senator's son was that nobody in the Oklahoma branch of the Coltons planned to go public with anything. Ever.

"Jesse," Rand Colton said, walking around from behind his desk, his right hand extended in greeting. "Or should I say, *cousin?*"

Jesse took the man's hand in his, felt the dry warmth and solid strength he hadn't expected to find in the grip of a lawyer. "Jesse's fine," he said, then took a seat on a chair that was part of a small conversational gathering of chairs and couch on one side of the large office. "Are we really sure?"

"You've spoken to your family?" Rand asked, lowering his six-foot-two-inch frame into the facing chair.

"Yes, when I went home after my grandmother's funeral. I couldn't be there in July, as I was traveling in Europe with the president, but I finally got there. They've been having some pretty interesting times in Black Arrow."

"Thanks to my uncle, yes," Rand said, shaking his head, then looking toward the now-open door. "Is there something wrong, Sylvia?"

"Oh, no sir, Mr. Colton. I only wondered if you and Mr. Colton might like some coffee," the secretary said.

"Coffee?" Rand asked, looking at Jesse.

"Sure," he answered, and turned to smile at the secretary. "I take it black, thank you."

"Oh, no trouble, Mr. Colton," Sylvia gushed, and Jesse saw a slight flush in her cheeks. "Really. It's absolutely no trouble at all."

As the secretary turned to exit, and nearly collided with the doorjamb, Rand said, "Do you always have that impact on women? I doubt I'll get any coffee at all. You'll probably get coffee *and* doughnuts."

Jesse settled himself in his chair once more, and grinned. "It's my Comanche blood, I suppose. Some women find that exciting."

"I find that Comanche blood interesting, frankly," Rand said, crossing one long leg over the other. "From everything I've learned about Teddy Colton—our mutual paternal grandfather—he was a heavy drinker, a social climber, a pompous ass—and a world-class bigot.''

"I really wouldn't know," Jesse said, resting his arms on the chair. "But I've seen early photographs of my grandmother just before she went to Reno to get a job that would allow her to send money home to her parents, and she was a beautiful woman. I mean, truly beautiful. He probably couldn't help himself.''

"I can believe that. I can also believe that Teddy met her and married her—before his society marriage to my grandmother. My paternal granddaddy, a bigamist. It's still mind-boggling. Have you seen the documentation?''

Jesse nodded. "On my visit home, yes. I brought the deed and marriage license back with me so I could look into the matter here. Although why Gloria—my grandmother—never told her sons the full truth is still beyond me.''

"Pride," Rand said with a slight nod of his head. "The way I've heard it, thanks to my father, is that when she realized she was pregnant and contacted Teddy, it was to learn that my grandmother was also pregnant. She could have raised one hell of a stink but she didn't. She just went home to raise her twin sons on her own. I admire her greatly. A simple woman with real class and a giving heart. Teddy, on the other hand, didn't trust her.''

"Never measure others by the length of your own lodgepole, as my great-grandfather would say. Teddy would have used information like that as a hammer, and so he felt sure Gloria would, as well. But she never did.''

"And she never took a penny from the trust Teddy set up in her name," Rand said, "or from the house he put into the trust for her. The Chekagovian embassy. I've already asked the lawyers who handle the trust to request that the embassy be vacated, and that's well in hand."

"I can't believe we can evict the Chekagovians," Jesse said with a smile.

"We didn't have to. It seems the embassy was already in the process of being emptied in favor of a newer building closer to the Capitol. It should be entirely vacant by the end of next week. I'll make sure you have keys waiting for you at the lawyers' office, as I'm sure you'll want to see the place. I know I would. Say, next Friday?"

Jesse lowered his eyelids, thinking that Samantha would be pleased when he told her he could take her on a tour of the estate. Nothing like turning this entire thing into a dating opportunity. He blinked, ordered his mind to concentrate on the matters at hand.

"Thank you. And about the trust? I'm still having a hard time getting my mind wrapped around that number. Ten million dollars?"

"Rounded down, yes. Sixty years of interest is a lot of interest, especially when the stock market began taking off—and especially when the trust was handled well enough to get out of that market and into safer funds while it was still high," Rand said, grinning. "And imagine. If my uncle Graham hadn't gotten greedy, nobody might have known about any of this."

"Yes, how did that happen?"

Rand and Jesse both stood up as Sylvia entered, carrying a tray holding a small pot, two cups and saucers and one plate of doughnuts. "Thank you, Sylvia. Sylvia?" Rand prompted as his secretary continued to stare at Jesse.

"Thank you, Sylvia," Jesse said, and the secretary blushed again, then backed her way out of the room.

"Truly amazing. I believe it's called charisma, Jesse," Rand said as he sat down once more. "Living in this town, you ought to run for office. You'd certainly get the female vote, if Sylvia's any indication."

"I'll keep that in mind," Jesse said, then took a bite of the glazed doughnut he'd selected.

"Anyway," Rand said, picking up his coffee cup, "it was Graham, my father's brother, who contacted our lawyers here in some desperation, wanting to sell up anything that might be left of their father and mother's estate."

"Yes, I remember the name now. Graham. The younger brother?"

"That's him. Graham earns plenty working for my dad, but money just runs through his fingers, so he was looking for another way to make a quick buck. The way I heard it, some junior law clerk, God knows why, mentioned the Georgetown mansion. Never should have happened because my grandfather had apparently explicitly demanded the estate be kept private unless the inquisitor had the deed in hand. Anyway, the clerk was disciplined, although I'm rather glad he made the mistake, if not happy how Graham reacted to learning of your grandmother's existence. He went ballistic, thinking about the money and the possible scandal."

"So you don't mind any of this?"

Rand shook his head. "The money simply isn't an issue. As for the scandal? It's ancient history. Besides, if the news had come out years ago, when Dad was running for the Senate, I imagine his handlers would have put a hell of a spin on it. Who knows, he could have ended up as president."

Jesse laughed, as did Rand. "My family met your father in Black Arrow. They were very impressed with him. Even my great-grandfather, and let me tell you, the old boy isn't an easy sell."

"Dad's good at impressing people. It comes naturally to him, probably because he's a good man. I wish I could say the same for Graham."

"He's the one who hired somebody to find the marriage license, birth certificates, the deed to the Georgetown mansion, and destroy them? The same guy who ordered the town hall burnt down?"

"Not to mention the break-ins at the newspaper office and your late grandmother's feed and grain store, yes. Busy, busy, busy. Although Graham swears he never told his hireling to do any of that. No violence, he told the guy, or so he says. Just to find the papers and destroy them, as if destroying evidence and robbing a family of its just inheritance were forgivable. But that's Graham. He sees things his own way. Luckily, the documents were always in a locked box in your grandmother's bedroom."

"And the lawyers here have verified everything from the original deed for the Georgetown property to the marriage license," Jesse said, perhaps a bit too sternly.

"Your whole branch of the Colton family is quite legitimate. You can rest assured that nobody on our side of the family is going to oppose your claim in any way.''

''Thank you. And I can tell you that no one on our side of the family is going to look this gift horse in the mouth, or try to profit from a sad situation by going public with it.''

Rand seemed relieved by his last statement. ''Sounds like we've agreed, then. Good, and I thank you. So, what do you and your family plan to do with the estate? With all that money?''

Jesse grinned, looked quite boyish for a moment. ''We haven't the faintest damn idea, cousin.''

Samantha ate at her desk, some quite wonderful beef sandwiches left over from the Sunday roast.

She knew the meat was good; it had been a nearly perfect rump roast she'd prepared with garlic mashed potatoes and freshly steamed broccoli. Rose, the live-in maid, who was a full-time student and the only staff Samantha would allow her mother to put in the house, had sworn it tasted like ambrosia. Samantha had agreed.

Yet, today, it tasted like cardboard.

She lifted the top piece of bread and stared at the meat, lettuce and mayonnaise. Nope. Not cardboard.

''Damn,'' she said, closing the sandwich once more and putting it back down on the desk.

''Something wrong?'' Bettyann entered the office and put some papers down on Samantha's desk, then deposited her rounded rump there as well.

''Nothing I'd want the media alerted for,'' Samantha

said, and watched as Bettyann blushed to the roots of her dyed blond hair.

"What…what does that mean?" the secretary asked, looking so guilty Samantha was surprised to not see the woman's hand stuck wrist-deep in a cookie jar.

"It means, Bettyann, that someone was here yesterday, asking questions about me, and you answered them."

"I did? What did I say?"

Samantha shook her head. Some things just weren't worth the effort. "Nothing, forget it."

"No, really," Bettyann said, standing up once more, and leaning her hands on the desktop. "Did I say something I shouldn't have said? And who did I say it to?"

"I'm not sure. Some secretary. Do you remember someone asking questions about me?"

Bettyann shook her head. "No. I do remember someone—a woman—coming in here yesterday, asking questions about everyone. You know, run-of-the-mill gossip. What it's like to work here, how are the bosses—stuff like that. I thought she was thinking of applying for the job we advertised last week. You know, sort of feeling us out without actually handing us a résumé? Why? Was it a reporter? Oh, cripes, Samantha, please tell me it wasn't a reporter."

"It wasn't a reporter," Samantha assured her. "Still, Bettyann, in the future, please try not to be so helpful to strangers, okay?"

"No, not okay. I shouldn't have said anything. I'm really, really sorry."

"I know. But we're getting closer and closer to New Hampshire, Bettyann, and the magnifying glass is being applied everywhere, including this office. I've been working on a memo directed to all staff, concerning questions that may come into the office. A sort of protocol to follow. I should have done it sooner.''

Bettyann grinned. ''Oh, good, it's your fault. I knew it wasn't my fault.''

''Spoken like a true politician. Get out of here,'' Samantha said on a laugh, and watched as Bettyann, hips exaggeratedly wiggling, left the office.

Once the secretary was gone, Samantha rewrapped her half-eaten sandwich and shoved it back into the navy-blue thermal bag she'd brought from home. Maybe she'd be hungry later, although she doubted it.

After Jesse Colton showed up, and looked at the papers locked in her bottom drawer? Maybe then she'd eat. Or she'd never be able to eat again.

Three hours later, while considering designs for a new series of campaign buttons, Samantha looked up at a knock on her opened office door.

She put down the buttons and stood up, then walked around the desk to give the well-dressed brunette a hug. ''Aunt Joan, what brings you to the salt mines?''

Mrs. Mark Phillips bestowed an air kiss on Samantha, then stepped back to look around the cluttered office. ''Oh, my. Time to get the bulldozers in here again, my dear,'' she said as Samantha quickly moved a stack of files from the only other chair and motioned for the senator's wife to sit down.

Joan Phillips was in her early fifties, but good genes and even better plastic surgery had her looking like a well-preserved forty. Or less.

Dark hair, marvelous blue eyes, skin the consistency of cream. A figure that flattered her designer suits. Jewels glittering on her hands and at her throat and ears, but discreetly, and half of them heirlooms that whispered rather than screamed "old money." A cultured voice, the ability to look adoringly at her husband as he made the same stump speech for the fiftieth time.

In short, Joan Phillips was the perfect candidate's wife.

Joan bent down and picked up the "Calm Day Across America" advertisement proposal Samantha had fashioned into an airplane and soared across the office...which was about as far as she thought it should go.

"Is this an editorial comment, or were you just playing?" the senator's wife asked, unfolding the makeshift airplane and reading the copy.

Samantha smiled. "I'll let you decide after you read it, okay?"

"Well, that must have taken at least two seconds of thought," Joan Phillips said after a moment, and then she refolded the page, sent it soaring toward the most distant corner of the room. "Did they come up with anything better than that, I most sincerely hope?"

"I've narrowed it down to two, yes, and I'll send those over for you and the senator to make the final decision. Or would you like to see them now?"

"No, no, not now. There's plenty of time for that when Mark and I are alone. I don't want to make up my mind without his input."

"Okay," Samantha said, wishing she didn't feel so nervous. Clumsy. All those bad things she always felt when in the presence of the neatly put-together Mrs. Mark Phillips.

It had always been that way, since she'd been a child. Uncle Mark was a doll, a peach. And his wife was lovely, ambitious. Very, very perfect.

Samantha always felt as if her own hair had to be messy and tangled, her blouse missing a button, her panty hose laddered with runs, whenever she was in Joan's presence. The woman didn't mean to make Samantha, or anyone, feel uncomfortable, but that perfection of hers could be intimidating to those who had to deal with her day to day in any official capacity.

To the public, she was just perfect. Pretty, friendly, articulate…even hip.

"Um…so…what does bring you down here, Aunt Joan?" Samantha asked when the silence became uncomfortable. For her, not for Joan. Joan was never uncomfortable.

"Well, dear, to tell you the truth, I just came to use the postal machine for some correspondence your uncle Mark and I want sent out. Is that what it's called? A postal machine? You know, that machine that marks envelopes with postage so that there's no need for stamps?"

"Close enough," Samantha said with a smile. "Would you like me to arrange to have one purchased for your home office? It would be more convenient for you."

"No, that's all right. I'm just as happy for an excuse to come see you and all our eager volunteers, dear. Besides, I have an appointment to have my nails done in a half hour." She reached into the lizard-skin briefcase she'd carried into the room with her and pulled out several flat, brown envelopes. "I'll just have someone stamp the postage on these and then I'll be out of your way."

"Oh, I'll do that," Samantha said, coming around the desk to take the envelopes from the woman.

"Really? Goodness, we don't pay you enough, dear. Thank you."

Samantha's heart was pounding as she accepted the envelopes.

And that's what they were. Envelopes, just envelopes. Four brown envelopes, the size needed to slip a typewritten page inside without folding it. Didn't all envelopes look alike? Of course they did.

Samantha put them on the desk behind her, then sort of blocked them with her body as she asked, "Is the president still deciding whether or not he'll be able to attend the fund-raiser next week?"

Joan rolled her eyes. "You know him, always trying to be the center of attention. Will he, won't he? I told your uncle Mark to announce that some Broadway cast, or one of those popular boy bands, or somebody like that would be there to perform. Entertainers always mean more media coverage. That would get Jackson to the affair, you could count on that, humming 'Hail To the Chief' to himself all the way."

"The whole world would want to be there if we could get that sort of entertainment, Aunt Joan. Even the opposition. But this isn't going to be that big a do, you know. Just two hundred of Uncle Mark's closest friends and supporters. Individuals. Nothing corporate.

Nothing to excite or upset anyone. We're just getting our feet wet.''

"Nonsense, Samantha. Your uncle has been raising funds on a daily basis for all of his three terms in the Senate. It's what has to be done. Only two hundred people? He doesn't need something small to get his feet wet. We're in fund-raising up to our ears, and have been since the beginning. You know as well as I that money for this presidential bid has been collecting in the proper accounts for almost two years. How else are we able to underpay you so badly, hmm? Now, who do you have for entertainment?''

"I'm...um...I'm still considering several options,'' Samantha said, desperately running through the file cabinet in her brain, wondering who she could call at the last moment, because she had not booked any entertainment.

"Well, good, then it's not to worry, is it?'' Joan said, getting to her feet in one fluid, graceful movement. "I must be off, I'm afraid. A stop at the salon, and then we have a dinner with several members of the party's California Primary Committee tonight at seven. We all know a candidate, to be viable, has to carry California. Have to plan ahead, right?''

"Definitely, and we're already polling well there, I'm happy to say,'' Samantha agreed, following Joan Phillips out of the office and through the central room that was loud with ringing telephones, clicking computer keys and the general babble of any office. "I'll...I'll be sure to get those envelopes in the mail for you, Aunt Joan. You said they were from both you and Uncle Mark?''

"Did I? Oh, yes, of course. Although we all know that, to your uncle, we're all errand boys, happy to do his bidding. Mine, his, ours, what does it matter? We must send out mail by the ton. Maybe I will take you up on that offer of one of those postal machines, dear. Except then I wouldn't get to see you so often, now, would I?"

With another exchange of air kisses, Joan Phillips was gone, and Samantha, after heaving a relieved sigh, was heading back into her office, carefully closing and locking the door behind her.

She spent the next two hours with a phone pressed to her ear, trying to round up some sort of entertainment that would follow the thousand-dollar-a-plate fund-raiser. As she dialed, then was put on hold, she pushed the envelopes Joan had left around her desktop with the eraser tip of a pencil.

She wanted to keep her distance, just in case one of them tried to bite her.

No return address, not on any of the envelopes. Just like the envelope locked in her bottom drawer. Computer-printed address labels, and all the addresses post office boxes, again just like the envelope locked in her bottom drawer.

Could she open the envelopes? Was that legal? There weren't any stamps on them yet, so it wasn't as if she'd be tampering with the U.S. mail.

Technically.

But it would be a breach of trust. Uncle Mark's trust in her. Her trust in him.

After two long, frustrating hours, Samantha had wrangled a gratis appearance at the fund-raiser out of

a popular female country-music trio, promising their
agent that the media coverage would be "substantial."
Three very pretty girls; talented, and they wore skimpy
costumes. That alone ought to make that thousand-
dollar-a-plate rubber chicken go down easier.

But she still didn't know what to do with the envelopes. Five of them now. Fairly bulky.

No wonder her aunt Joan, known to be tight with a
penny so she could spend lots of dollars, hadn't wanted
to trust licking the correct amount of stamps. With only
a post office box address, and no return address, the
envelopes would end up in the dead letter office if the
postage wasn't sufficient.

So much more efficient to use the postal machine in
the campaign office.

Except that, Samantha knew, as a senator, Uncle
Mark could send out all the official mail he wanted via
his office, and at no charge.

So this wasn't official mail. Without the return address, it probably wasn't campaign literature, either.

So what was in these other envelopes? More of what
she'd found in the first one?

It was that last thought, the one that had been nag-
ging at her all afternoon, that had Samantha unlocking
the bottom drawer and sliding the four envelopes into
it, on top of the first envelope.

Jesse checked his watch for the second time in as
many minutes. Was he already too late? He should
have known he wouldn't get out of the office at a reasonable hour. Reasonable, in his line of work, meant
anywhere between six and eight. Face it, reasonable

quitting times, for those working in the West Wing, were a joke.

It was now almost nine, and he had chosen to jog over to Phillips's campaign headquarters rather than take his car and spend another twenty minutes hunting up a parking space.

He stopped outside the office building and looked up. Second floor. Yes, there were still lights on, which meant that Samantha was there, waiting for him.

Probably with her lovely slim, coral-tipped fingers drawn up into fists. Pacing, cursing him, second-guessing herself for having contacted him in the first place.

No matter what, he was pretty certain he wasn't going to be greeted as if he'd brought the flowers of May along with him. Not when she was so nervous about whatever the hell she thought was so important about the mail she'd discovered.

He walked past the elevator and climbed the stairs two at a time, stripping off his black raincoat and mussing his hair enough that, he hoped, he didn't look like a SSST—Stereotypical Secret Service Type.

The last thing he wanted to look was official on this visit, in any way.

He walked into the office, surprised to see so many people still there, talking on phones, licking envelopes and examining poll numbers chalked on a large board.

First, he thought with a small smile, you work your buns off to get into the office, and then you work your buns off to stay there. First the small, crowded office, the Styrofoam white boater hats with the red, white and blue ribbons on them, the campaign jingles, the stale doughnuts and sore ears from spending their lives on the phone. Then the win, and a move to the OEOB, or maybe even the West Wing, and even longer hours for less satisfaction, not as many wins.

And no nifty Styrofoam boater hats.

Campaign workers were like hamsters running on one of those endless wheels, always running, never really getting anywhere. They just believed they did.

A blonde badly in need of a dye job walked past, reading a fax, and Jesse put out his arm to stop her. "Excuse me, but is Ms. Cosgrove available?"

The blonde looked up, blinked, and then put one hand on her hip. "If she's not, I am. Bettyann Muldoon, at your service. And I do mean that literally."

Jesse smiled one of his aw-shucks grins. "Thank you, ma'am, but I really do need to see Ms. Cosgrove."

"Ma'am? Oh, boy, now I know I'm past it. What's next, I ask you, orthopedic shoes?" Bettyann said, grimacing. "Well, I guess I might as well start acting like I've read the latest memo, huh?"

"And I'll pretend as if I know what you're talking about, okay? In any case, go for it, Bettyann," Jesse said, still grinning.

"Thank you. Here goes." She stood up taller and said in a patently fake official-sounding voice, "I'm so sorry, sir, but I don't believe I got your name. Do you have an appointment to see Ms. Cosgrove?"

"Not an appointment, not in the penciled-in-at-nine sort of appointment anyway, but she is expecting me. Perhaps she mentioned me? Jesse Colton?"

"Oh, so this is *personal*?" Bettyann asked, looking

as if she might pull out a pen and paper and begin taking notes.

"You could say that," Jesse told her, giving her another grin. This one not so shy and boyish.

"Hot damn, it's about time that girl got out and about. You just stay here, Mr....um...Mr....oh, just stay here, okay? I'll go get her."

Jesse busied himself looking around the large, square room, admiring the huge, smiling-faced reproduction of Senator Mark Phillips's handsome, even distinguished face plastered on one wall from floor to ceiling.

Red, white and blue bunting was everywhere, along with the requisite number of flags, the autographed photograph of Phillips with the president, taken in the Oval Office, and another of the senator and his charming wife posed on a rocky beach.

The atmosphere in the room was barely controlled pandemonium, and Jesse decided that he could probably work in this office for oh, five minutes, before the top of his head blew clean off.

Into this mess strode Samantha Cosgrove, the dye-job blonde trailing in her wake.

Samantha looked like the calm in the middle of the storm, the serene princess who kept her cool while everyone else ran around bumping into each other like the cast of a *Three Stooges* reprise.

He could have kissed her.

Hey, wait a moment. Why couldn't he kiss her?

"Samantha," he said, stepping toward her just as she opened her mouth, probably to tell him to go away, come back later, when the madness had died down.

Fat chance.

"Hello, baby," he crooned as he drew her into his arms, and he got a quick peek at Bettyann just before he claimed Samantha's mouth.

The secretary's eyes opened so wide that if someone hit her on the back of the head, both orbs might just have popped out, rolled away on the floor.

But that didn't matter. What mattered was that Samantha's mouth was everything he'd dreamed of through a long, nearly sleepless night. Warm, soft. Like her body. Warm, soft.

Her mouth tasted so good.

How would the rest of her taste?

She began to struggle, but not obviously, so that someone would come to her assistance. Oh, no. Samantha Cosgrove was too much the lady to do anything obvious. What she did was put her hands up to either side of his neck, then push her thumbnails into the crease directly behind each of his ears.

It did smart. It definitely did smart. He'd have to tell the guys at Quantico about the move, and they could add it to their One Thousand Nifty Ways to Disarm an Adversary handbook.

He pulled back his head just slightly and smiled down at her.

"What in hell do you think you're doing?" she asked. But she whispered.

"I'm kissing you hello," he explained, also in a whisper. And then he kissed her again, on the side of the throat, so that he could be even closer to her ear. "Think, Samantha. Nobody can know I'm here on official business, right? I thought you'd be the only one here."

"Oh. I hadn't thought of that. Okay. But you can let me go now. Please?"

"I don't want to," he said honestly.

"Tough beans," she answered, and when he dropped his arms in surprise, she stepped away from him.

"I take it you know Jesse James here?" Bettyann asked Samantha, jerking a thumb at him. "Man. If I could keep a secret like that, I'd have to wonder why."

"Go away, Bettyann," Samantha said, but she smiled as she said it. "Oh, and why not take everyone else with you. There's really nothing more anyone can do tonight about those new poll numbers."

"Are you sure? We dropped six points. If the newspapers were to find out about our private poll…? I mean, are you sure?" Bettyann was still looking at Jesse.

"Positive. And there will be a new set of numbers next week. I've checked, and New Hampshire is known for doing this sort of thing, right up until the primary. I think they like the attention they get when the outcome is still up in the air. But they're savvy voters, Bettyann, very well informed, so the senator will win when the votes really count. But remember, those numbers are confidential, and not for public consumption, should anyone ask."

"Spoken like a true, loyal campaign worker," Jesse said, walking with Samantha toward her open office door. "Did he lose his lead? The president wouldn't like that."

"No, he didn't lose his lead, but he's dropped out of a double-digit lead for the moment. And you weren't supposed to hear *any* of that," she told him, closing the door behind them, then turned to look at him, shake her head. "Bettyann seems to have this problem."

"A problem?"

"Yes. Her mouth. She opens it *way* too much."

"Filled peppers?" Jesse asked, grinning at her.

"Exactly. She trusts everybody. She trusted your secretary, probably because she's one of those innocent-looking types. I mean, you wouldn't have used her if she would have come in here swirling her cape and looking like the female half of Boris and Natasha, now, would you? And now Bettyann trusted you just because you're gorgeous—oh, damn! Never mind that last part."

"Are you kidding? I'm never going to forget it. So, you think I'm gorgeous?"

"No," Samantha said, rolling her eyes. "Bettyann thinks you're gorgeous. She also thinks your name is Jesse James, so don't be too flattered, okay? Now, do you want to see what I've got or not?"

"Now *there's* a line I could interpret in many wonderful ways."

"Oh, shut up."

"Touchy. I probably have to feed you again." Jesse looked around the small, cluttered office. "This place doesn't look anything like you. I'd pictured chrome and glass and…oh, I don't know. Order?"

"I work well in clutter," Samantha said, seating herself behind the desk. "What I don't work well in is being the center of office gossip. You do realize that now that everyone thinks you're my boyfriend, all I'll get are questions about you? And then sympathy, once you're gone again. Just what I've always wanted to be, the lovesick gal dropped by the gorgeous man. I can hear Bettyann now, looking all sad-eyed and sorry, constantly asking if I want to 'talk about it.' Yippee.''

He walked over to one corner, peeked under the shade of a floor lamp. ''One public kiss makes me your boyfriend?''

''Around here, yes. Or have you forgotten that Washington is the birthplace of more gossip than even Hollywood? By tomorrow morning they'll have us picking out china patterns. It's disgusting.''

''So now we have to get married?'' Jesse asked, just because Samantha was blushing, and she looked really cute when she blushed. Not so sleek, so sophisticated. More touchable. Definitely touchable. He looked up at the ceiling light, an old-fashioned chandelier type, but fortunately very plain in its design. Nope. He didn't see anything there.

''Sure, why not,'' she said, pulling a small key from her purse. ''I'd like three children, I believe. Two boys and a girl.''

''Glad to hear you have this all figured out.'' Jesse went down on his hands and knees, ran one hand along the underside of a folding worktable stacked with manila folders and campaign bumper stickers.

He moved his hand slowly, carefully. And then he felt it. He stuck his head under the table, took a good look. *Bingo!* He stood up once more, moved away from the table. ''Two boys and a girl, you say? I'll have to work on that. Can we start tonight? I mean, hey, tonight's good for me.''

She was looking at him as if he'd just set his own

hair on fire. "You're impossible, as well as hopelessly optimistic. We're meeting here, Jesse, because I didn't want to meet you anywhere else. Understand? And what are you doing?"

He put one finger over his lips, then pulled a small notebook from his pocket and borrowed a pen from the cup on her desk. Scribbled a few words, handed the note to her.

"Do I understand? That's what you asked? If I understood?" he asked as she read the note. "I think *you* also need to understand, darling."

She looked at him as if he'd penned "There's a great big bomb in here and it detonates in five, four, three, two—oops, too late!"

He grinned at her as she continued to goggle at him, and then spoke again before she could so much as open her mouth. "Well, to be clearer, I think I do understand what you think you understand. To you, this is strictly business, your effort to turn me into a rabid Phillips for President advocate. It's probably going to take days, even weeks, before you'll admit how much you love me."

"How much I love you? What are you talking about? I want to talk about—"

He shook his head, kept talking. "Gee, that's too bad. And here I was, all ready to ask you if you wanted to tour the Georgetown mansion next Friday. That, and to convince you that you don't just want me as a Phillips supporter. You're hot for my body."

Samantha was still looking at him as she repeatedly pointed to the note he'd written. "You're kidding."

She hadn't even heard him make that hot-for-his-body crack. Pity. He would have liked to have heard her response.

"I said," she repeated, "you're kidding, right?"

He shook his head. "Kidding? I'll have you know, Ms. Cosgrove, that I am loyal, and trustworthy, very often discreet, and still suffer from that George Washington complex. No, I'm not kidding. The current tenants are leaving for new quarters, and the place will be empty next Friday, at which time I—good person who never lies—get the key. The key, darling. So, are you interested?"

She held up the key that *she* already had in her hand, then frowned at him in question.

Good girl. She was scared, but she wasn't slow on the uptake. She knew what he wanted, why he'd mentioned the key.

He nodded, and Samantha nodded back at him as he picked up the note he'd written and slid it into the pocket of his suit jacket.

She opened the drawer, pulled out a stack of brown envelopes and slammed them down on the desktop. "You know I'm interested. In the house, Jesse, not you. Whatever we had, it's over, gone, *kaput*. Do you hear me?"

As she said those last words, she spoke directly at the folding table.

He gave an exaggerated sigh. He had to keep this light, keep it silly, if possible. Just two young lovers having a spat; nothing anyone would spend much time listening to, or try to decipher. "Ah, sweetheart. There goes your membership in the George Washington I Cannot Tell a Whopper Club. I mean, when you were kissing a guy out there in the outer office? I was the guy. And you were interested."

"Maybe," she said, sorting through the envelopes, pulling out the bottom one, the open one. She held up one finger, then all five, and looked at him questioningly. "You *are* kind of cute, in a pathetic sort of way."

He held up five fingers. Hey, she said one, but if she had more than one, he wanted all of them. "Gorgeous. You said I was gorgeous."

Samantha wet her lips with the tip of her tongue. She was nervous, sure, but she was also great. Coming along like gangbusters, as if she did this all the time. He smiled encouragingly at her. "I did not call you gorgeous," she said. "Bettyann did. I thought you smart guys knew how to keep your facts straight."

"We also know how to bend the facts so that they sound good, better than they really are. So, what about me do you find gorgeous? My eyes? My chin? My engaging smile? My scintillating repartee? Tell me how you love me. Let's count the ways."

Samantha stood up and glared at him across the desktop. "Would you please stop that."

"Not until you tell me that you love me."

As he said the words, he pointed to the folding table just to remind her. Whoever could hear them had to think they were lovers not conspirators. "Say it." He slowly, silently mouthed the words *I...love...you.*

She blinked, then swallowed hard as she absorbed those three words. "I loved you yesterday," she said at last, opening her briefcase and putting all five of the envelopes inside, closing it again. "Today I think you're nuts."

"Ah, another of my sterling features. I'm nuts. Speaking of nuts, are you hungry? I sure could do with some spaghetti, or maybe some Chinese?"

"I've got leftover roast beef at home, and some garlic mashed potatoes."

"Beef good, garlic bad, especially with what I have in mind, darling," Jesse said, motioning for her to come out from behind the desk.

She did, but then she stopped next to the folding table, bent down and looked at the underside of the thing.

Two seconds later, she was standing again, and her gorgeous blue eyes were open very wide. "Did you— do you *see*—"

Well, there was nothing else he could do, was there? She'd been great, a real brick, but now she was having a minor meltdown, and she was going to blow the whole thing. He had no choice. He had to kiss her again.

It might not have been part of his training as an agent, shutting someone up this way, but he was always open to learning new things.

Chapter Three

Very high on Samantha's to-do list was getting Jesse Colton to kiss her again. Definitely.

But it wasn't number one.

It couldn't be.

The moment they were outside the office building, she grabbed his arm, half spun him around and whispered hoarsely, "A *bug?* My office is *bugged?* Who? How? *Why?*"

Jesse ran a fingertip down her cheek. "You're cute when you're panic-stricken."

"Oh, shut up," she said, rapidly walking ahead of him down the wide pavement. Then she stopped. "Wait. Where are we going?"

"That depends, I suppose. My car's back at the lot. Where's yours?"

"Closer. We have our own lot out back. I'll drive you to yours. And then we're going somewhere to talk."

"I thought I'd been invited home to dinner?"

Samantha frowned as they turned the corner, headed for the back of the building. "Did I do that? I can't remember much at the moment."

"You did it, sweetheart. I accepted the roast beef, rejected the garlic mashed potatoes. Ring any chords in your memory?"

No, she thought. She was pretty sure her memories would pretty much concentrate on his mouthing the words *I love you,* and then kissing her. Again.

Even more, her dreams would be haunted by his words when she told him to let her go: "I don't want to."

The man had a way with words....

She shook herself out of her definitely mushy mood. "Too bad about the potatoes, because I'm having them."

"In that case, so will I. Well, that's one problem solved. Now, where did you park?"

She pressed a hand to her forehead and looked around the parking lot. Where had she parked her car? She *had* driven to work, right?

Now, *there* was a thought she should have had sooner.

Samantha looked at him, felt her cheeks growing hot. "I remember now. I took the Metro this morning."

"Easy enough to forget," Jesse said, swinging her around so that they were heading in the direction of the parking deck where his sedan waited. "After all, you've had an interesting few minutes."

She nodded as she did a quick double-step to keep

up with his long strides. "Bugged. I can't believe this. Who'd do that?"

"Well, for starters, the bug isn't government issue. That rules out a lot."

"So I'm not under some federal investigation?"

"I don't think so. But that leaves some even more uncomfortable conclusions."

"Name one."

"Okay. The opposition. It's a stretch, but dumb has been done before. Then there's the question of who rented the space before you guys moved in. This could be a leftover bug, inoperative now, from someone who'd been listening in on the last tenants."

Samantha liked that idea a lot. "Yes, that could be it. That has to be it. A leftover bug, one they missed when they cleaned out all the other bugs. Do you think there could be other bugs?"

"You like that scenario, do you? It's Washington, sweetheart, so we'll say scenario. It sounds so official."

"Would you just shut up and tell me what you think, please?"

"Ah, the lady has a temper. Okay, okay, how about this one? Your own people have bugged their own campaign office. You know, just to keep themselves informed about everything that goes on?"

Samantha stopped dead on the sidewalk. "No," she said, her heart pounding. "Uncle Mark wouldn't do that."

"Which answers my next question. You're not going to ask him, are you?"

"Ask him! Are you nuts? Are you out of your mind? I can't *ask* him."

"Probably not," Jesse said as they entered the parking deck. "Besides, I really should check out the bug more, make sure it is active. We can do that tomorrow night, after hours. I just need a few pieces of equipment, especially since I want to check for more listening devices."

"Yes, that's another thing. Why did you check? Do you know something I don't know?"

"Volumes, darling, when it comes to this kind of stuff," he said, his smile taking any sting out of his words. "And I don't know why I checked. Just a natural response for someone with my training, I guess. Little kids check under the bed for ogres, and I check everywhere else for listening devices, hidden cameras, all kinds of goodies."

"Well…thank you. I think," Samantha said as he held open the passenger-side door for her and she slipped inside. This time she let her raincoat fall open and gave him a glimpse of knee. He deserved that, at the least.

He started the car and backed out of the parking space, headed for the exit. "You didn't answer me. Do you know who the last tenant was in your office?"

"I don't know, no, but I don't have to know, because I just remembered something else. I bought that table. It wasn't in my office when we moved in."

"That's not good news."

"Duh," Samantha said, rolling her eyes. "Oh, I'm sorry, I didn't mean to be nasty," she said a moment later. "I'm…I'm pretty stressed right now."

"And still very pretty, sweetheart," Jesse said, reaching over to pat her arm. "I kind of like how you forgot you took the Metro to work this morning."

She nodded. "Yes. I couldn't find my car keys. I have an extra set, but for some strange reason I keep those in my office desk."

"Is that so?" Jesse said, then shook his head slightly.

"Bugged," Samantha said in aid of nothing except her own inability to absorb this news.

They drove the rest of the way in silence, both wrapped up in private thoughts.

Jesse pulled into a clear spot a few doors down from her house and cut the engine, but when she moved to open the door he placed a restraining hand on her arm.

"What? Don't tell me you want me to wait for you to be a gentleman?"

"That, too, but first I want to ask you a question. Last night, when I brought you home, you searched in your purse for something, then rang to have your maid let you into the house. Why?"

Samantha sat back against the soft leather seat. "Why? Because I couldn't find my keys. I told you that."

"Okay, I was just laying background here. It helps me think. Now, tell me, what keys do you keep on that particular ring? House key, key to the car—anything else?"

She reached into her purse and came out with a burgundy leather key case that snapped shut over her ample store of keys, waved it at him. "Sure. The keys to the offices, the main one and mine. The key to my bike chain. The key to my desk drawers, the one to my files, the—oh, boy.''

"Exactly, sweetheart. Oh boy. But you had the keys tonight, right?''

She nodded. "I keep extra office keys, desk keys, hidden in Bettyann's desk, so I could work, but it was late this afternoon before Bettyann found my case on the floor next to the copy machine in the main office. I don't remember using the machine, but I must have, and then left them there.''

"Uh-huh.''

"What *uh-huh?* I don't think I like when you say uh-huh. Scratch that. I definitely don't like it when you say uh-huh. So, what uh-huh? What are you thinking?''

"Nothing,'' he said, but he said it too quickly for Samantha's comfort.

"Don't do that, Jesse. If you're thinking something, I want to know what something you're thinking.''

"Okay, here goes. Someone lifted your keys yesterday, and used them to get into the office last night.''

"To plant that bug?''

He shook his head. "No, I don't think so. That's probably been there for a while, maybe even since you first opened up shop. Maybe there's something wrong with the bug, and they needed to get in to fix it...or to plant something else. You didn't notice anything unusual, like on your desk, in your desk drawers? Did anything look out of place?''

She laughed without humor. "You *have* seen my office, haven't you? I wouldn't notice an elephant sitting smack in the middle of the room playing a fiddle.''

"True. They probably counted on that.''

"They counted on what? And who's *they?* Who counted on it?"

"Whoever borrowed your keys, Samantha. Don't panic, and stay with me on this, okay? Someone needed the key to your office, maybe even to your desk. They just happened to get your car key and house key, but what they probably wanted was your desk key. Tell me, have you kept those envelopes in that locked drawer all along?"

Samantha began biting on the side of her thumb, a nervous habit she thought she'd left behind her in the third grade. "Yes, that's where I put it last week. Those other envelopes just came in today, and I put them with the first one."

"I was going to ask about that. I thought you'd only said one envelope. Okay. So you took an envelope that was supposed to go out in the mail last week. The envelope doesn't arrive where it's supposed to, when it's supposed to, and someone comes to check out why. You with me so far?"

"Sort of. But what about the bug?"

"Amateur-hour stuff, I'm sure of it. The kind of thing you can buy mail order these days, when nobody trusts anybody else. We may be working with two entirely different things. Or just one person with a whacking-great paranoia problem."

"Uncle…you mean Senator Phillips? No, I can't see it. I just can't."

"You're loyal, Samantha, and that's nice. I, on the other hand, am suspicious of everyone. It's my training. That said," he continued, pulling the keys out of the ignition, "we're going into your house now, but we're not talking until I've at least given it a visual once-over for bugs. Your house key was missing all day and night, right?''

"Right. But I've got Rose."

"She was in the house all day yesterday?"

Samantha sighed. "No. Rose is also a full-time college student. She had a full boatload of classes yesterday. She only wears the uniform once in a while, as a joke, and to get a rise out of me—like when she has to take out the garbage. She keeps calling me the czarina and herself a prime example of the oppressed proletariat laboring class. She's majoring in Russian history, you understand."

"Cute. So she wasn't home? Still, we can't be sure. Do you have a security system?"

Samantha brightened. "Yes! We have a security system. How could I forget that? You have to punch in a code within so many seconds of unlocking the door and—oh, damn it!"

"Now, why do you suppose I'm thinking that the next thing you're going to say isn't going to make me happy?"

"This tears it. Mother and Dad find out and I'm home before I can pack. You know that, don't you? Juliet gets to run all over New York, and our brother is on his own at college, but not me. Oh, no. Not Samantha. Why do parents always pick one to keep on a shorter leash?"

He took her leather key case from her slack hand and opened it. "Oh, I don't know, Samantha. But if I were to hazard a guess, I'd say it might be because one of their kids just might think she's going to forget things like, say, a security code, and so she writes it down inside her key case with permanent black marker. How's that for a guess?''

"I hate you,'' she muttered, grabbing the key case from him. "If I give you a quarter, will you promise not to tell my parents?''

"If you give me a kiss, I won't even give you a lecture on security. At least not one that lasts more than about ten minutes. How's that?''

Samantha glared at him, then opened the car door. "Come on. I want you to see if there are any bugs in my house. Then I'll feed you, and then I'll show you the papers. After that, hey, buying me one dinner and finding a bug in my office do not count toward kissing privileges. You didn't even kill the bug for me.''

"I knew she'd get around to saying that one at some point,'' she overheard him grumble to himself before he, too, got out of the car.

Jesse spoke with Rose for about twenty minutes, the same amount of time it took for Samantha to go from looking great but professional to great but touchable.

Oh, boy. Definitely touchable.

When she reappeared downstairs, dressed in soft burgundy velour slacks and an ivory angora sweater with a large cowl collar, her blond hair pulled back in a casual ponytail at her nape, he was in the middle of one last question to Rose...a question which he promptly forgot.

"Yoo-hoo, still in there?'' Rose asked with a grin, waving a hand in front of Jesse's face. "Man, I wish I had that effect on men,'' the short brunette continued, making a face. "Heck, I'd settle for one man. And he could be bald, really. I'm not choosy."

"Oh, stop it, Rose," Samantha said. "I had to put a separate telephone line in here in order to be able to use the phone, because you get so many calls."

Rose beamed. "That's true. I'm a goddess. Okay, I'm fine now. It was a momentary lapse. I have those when she's around," she added, looking at Jesse while she hooked a thumb in Samantha's direction. "Hey, why am I telling you? You're one of the poleaxed, right? Because you sure looked it when she came down those stairs."

"Guilty as charged, Rose," Jesse said, winking at the girl. "She's a babe."

"Cut that out," Samantha protested, sitting down in a large green leather chair, tucking her bare feet up beside her on the seat cushion. "I can see Rose has found a kindred spirit in you. I probably should have a shield, or a sword, or something, just to make things even."

"Yeah, well, fun's fun and all that," Rose said, getting to her feet, "but the books are calling me. Rasputin. Now, *there* was a piece of work, let me tell you. Do you know how many times they had to kill him until he finally died? I mean, this is big stuff!"

"Go away, Rose," Samantha said, shaking her head, and Rose skipped out of the room.

"She's not really a maid, is she?" Jesse asked once the young woman was gone.

"Technically, she is. In reality, she rules me. But it was the only way Mother would let me move back here, so Rose moved in and earns her keep and I have someone to talk to, someone who'd call the police if I didn't come home one night and ask them to drag the river for my body. That sort of thing. My mother's a good egg, honest, but she has this tendency to think in potential tragedies.''

Jesse nodded. ''Mothers can be like that. I know, because I have one, too. Oh, and you were right. Rose was gone most of yesterday.''

Samantha leaned forward in her chair. ''Can we really talk here?''

''Yeah, it's okay, we're clear, at least in this room. Although you might want Rose to dust behind the couch if you don't think she'll give you a lecture on abuse of the working classes. I think the dust bunnies have begun to mate.''

''Funny.'' Samantha made a face at him. He loved when she did that. She went from looking like a sleek high-fashion model to being this cute, comic girl-woman. The kind who could make one hell of an entrance at a party in her designer gown, yet look just as good in a sweater and corduroys, rolling around in the fall leaves.

Man, he was getting hooked. He was really getting hooked.

''Anyway, I think we're pretty safe in assuming that nobody was in here. It's a lot neater here than in your office, and Rose didn't think anything was out of place. Still, I'll give it a much more thorough check tomorrow.''

''So whoever took my keys—if anyone took my keys—wanted them to get into my office, into my desk?''

"That would be my guess. Are you hungry?"

"Probably. But I'm still too upset. No, scratch that. I'm *angry*. I'm really, really angry."

Jesse understood. "The violation, right?"

"Yes, exactly. I feel as if I've been violated. Is that stupid?"

"Not at all. Now, how about we hit the kitchen and warm up those leftovers."

She got to her feet and led the way. "You don't mind leftovers?"

"Sweetheart," he said, "I don't mind any food that started out as home-cooked, trust me. I'd even eat it cold."

She turned to him in the narrow hallway leading to the kitchen. "Why do you do that?"

"Why do I do what?" She smelled good, really good. Like spring flowers.

"Call me sweetheart. Call me darling."

"I do?"

She gave him a small push in the chest. "You know darn full well you do."

"Hmm," he said as she continued into the small but perfect kitchen. "I'll have to think about this. Do you think it's subconscious?"

"No, I don't think it's subconscious," she told him, pulling containers of food out of the refrigerator. "I think you're very conscious of everything you do."

"In that case, should I stop?"

She hesitated, holding plastic containers in both hands. "Let me think about that."

Feeling pretty darn good about himself, Jesse took

the containers from her and she dived back into the refrigerator for two more.

"Sit," she said, taking the containers from him and motioning toward a heavy round oak table and ladder-back chairs. "This kitchen is too small for two people, or at least that's what Rose says when she wants to get out of kitchen duty."

Jesse decided that, where Samantha was concerned, he was nothing if not obedient. He sat down, cupped his chin in one hand and happily watched her swift, efficient movements as she loaded containers of food into the microwave, ripped some romaine for salad.

"You like to cook," he said, and it wasn't a question.

"I love it," she said, looking at him over her shoulder. "I used to haunt this kitchen, and then the one in Connecticut. The colors, the smells, the textures. Even the cleanup doesn't bother me. Rose is very grateful for that, and in exchange, she does all the washing and ironing. I think I got the better end of the bargain."

"I think Rose fell into a pile of more roses, myself," Jesse said, pulling two glasses from a glass-fronted cabinet and filling them with ice from the dispenser built into the front of the refrigerator. "Ice water? Something else?"

"There are cans of soda in the pantry—that long cabinet over there. I'd offer you wine, but I want to keep a clear head, and I think even a sip of wine, with me feeling the way I do now, would send me over the edge into full-blown hysteria."

Ten minutes later, they were sitting across from each other at the table, and Jesse was falling deeper into love. The roast beef was tender and tasty, the gravy thick and dark, and the garlic mashed potatoes were a gift from the gods he was glad he hadn't turned down.

"If your leftovers taste this good, tell me who I have to kill to be invited for Sunday dinner."

"I'm glad you like everything," Samantha said, looking both pleased and proud at his comment. "I'm a plain cook, but I'm a good cook, if I do say so myself. Now, how about we leave these dishes and go look at the envelope that first had me calling you for help."

"I thought you said you liked to clean up."

"No, sir, Mr. Colton, sir, I certainly did not say that. I said I don't mind. Nobody *likes* cleaning up. Oh, all right, let's do it. I swear, sometimes there are more dishes and containers just heating leftovers than there are in making a full dinner."

Jesse picked up his own dinner plate and salad bowl and headed for the sink. This felt good. Natural. Being in this cozy kitchen with Samantha Cosgrove. Doing simple, domestic things.

He suddenly wanted things he'd never wanted before. A home of his own. Kids sleeping upstairs.

Samantha.

He watched appreciatively as she bent over the dishwasher, loading the last of the dishes, then started the appliance. Some people might say Mount Rushmore had a great view. Others, the Grand Canyon.

He'd take this view, any day…

"So," she said, straightening, wiping her hands on a dish towel. "I guess we can't put this off any longer. Back to the living room?"

"Since I checked it out already, yes. And you know, you never told me what you found in that envelope."

"You never asked," she said, preceding him back down the hallway.

"That's because I figured you were overreacting, but if I found out you were, you'd say we didn't have to see each other anymore, and I wasn't ready for that. How's that for honest, sweetheart?"

She half stumbled over a Persian-style throw rug, then kept walking.

Once back in the living room, she removed the envelopes from her briefcase, handed them to him, and sat down in the green leather chair once more.

He picked the couch, a soft, chintz-covered affair that probably had been restuffed and recovered umpteen times. Good furniture was like that, he'd heard. Kept forever, recovered and restrung, and always as comfortable as an old slipper.

"This is a great room," he said, laying the envelopes in his lap. "Does that fireplace work?"

"It's gas, yes. Should I turn it on?"

Would he like to see Samantha's blond hair and clear features in firelight? Yeah, he could handle that. "I'll do it," he said, but when he was only halfway to his feet the fire had already gone on.

"How'd you do that?" he asked, subsiding again.

She held up a small remote control. "Magic," she said, and grinned. "Okay. Fire's on, room's been commented on. Can we get on with this before I burst?"

So she knew he'd been stalling. Hell, that wasn't a stretch. He'd already admitted why he'd been stalling. But, he would admit only to himself, there was also a part of him that couldn't wait to see the papers that had set off such an alarm in Samantha's mind.

"Do the open one first. That way, if it's nothing, we don't even have to look at the others, right?"

"Beautiful, a great cook, and logical, too," Jesse said, locating the open envelope and sliding out the ten or so pages it held.

He looked at the first page, then looked at Samantha.

Poor baby. She was staring at him, eyes wide, and biting on the side of her thumb again.

He looked back at the page, then turned to the next, quickly flipped to the next.

"Oh boy," he said at last, sitting back on the couch. "Do you know what this is?"

She nodded. "I do. At least I think I do. I think it's planned legislation for a possible targeted tax break to certain types of industries."

"It sure is. And it's committee-stage work, not for public consumption. Nobody knows about this yet. I mean, sure, the president probably knows, and the majority leader, and the committee heads, of course. But this is early stuff, supposition, trial balloon-type stuff. Sort of a feasibility test, to see if it could work, help the economy. If these industries knew what was being discussed in this memo, the lobbyists would be out in droves, covering the Capitol, wining and dining, hoping for votes."

"So it shouldn't have gone out in the mail," Samantha said, twisting her hands in her lap.

"Hell no," Jesse said, looking at the pages again. "These are internal notes, an internal memo, and just to the majority's side of the committee at that. I don't get it."

"Yes, you do," Samantha said, and she turned away from him, stared into the fire.

"Okay, yes I do. If I wanted to sell my vote to the highest bidder, I'd want companies involved in these industries to know I'm up for sale."

"Like, maybe, they could buy a friend in government by contributing, big time, to a certain senator's presidential election campaign?"

"Move that girl to the head of the class," Jesse said, shoving the papers back into the envelope.

"What are you going to do?"

Jesse was angry, and it took him a moment to realize that although Samantha might also be angry, she also had other problems. She worked for Senator Phillips. She was, at this point, a reluctant whistle-blower. Not anyone's favorite place to be in Washington, D.C.

"First," he said carefully, "I'm going to look at the rest of these envelopes, see what's in them. I see that each one is addressed to a different post office box. Five envelopes, five different cities and states. Maybe they all contain copies of that same memo?"

"Are you sure we can open them? I mean, aren't they U.S. mail?"

"Not yet. There are no stamps on them."

"That's splitting hairs, Jesse," she told him. "I did the same thing. But I have to tell you, I still feel guilty about it."

"Close your eyes, then, and don't look," Jesse said as he opened the first sealed envelope.

He opened the second, the third. Didn't bother with the fourth.

"Blank. Nothing but blank pages," he said as Samantha gnawed on the side of her thumb once more, realized what she was doing and immediately stopped.

"I don't get it. Why would Aunt Joan be sending out blank pages?"

Jesse laid the envelopes to one side. "Do the words *this is a test* sound at all familiar?"

"A test? Of who? Whom, I mean. I'm sure I mean whom. A test of whom?"

Jesse wasn't sure. He hated not being sure. "I don't know. A test of the delivery system? A test meant for you? Tell me again about Mrs. Phillips's visit today. Step by step, sweetheart, don't leave anything out."

She did as he asked, with amazing detail, all the way down to Joan Phillips's move with the discarded advertising copy, how she sent it winging into a corner of the room.

"Okay," he said when Samantha had finished speaking. "This is just off the top of my head, but here goes. One, Mrs. Phillips brought the envelopes into your office, walking past all the people in the outside office, the postage machine, you name it, to let you see the envelopes."

"That's true. She could have handed them to Bettyann. Or Rita. Anybody. She certainly didn't have to carry them into my office."

"Two," Jesse went on, getting into it now. "She diverted your attention throwing that paper airplane. You did follow its flight, right?"

"Right," Samantha said, nodding. "It was a short

flight, though, Jesse. I probably only took my eyes off her for a couple of seconds.''

"But she was sitting in the chair directly next to the worktable? The one with the bug stuck underneath it? It takes less than three seconds to place a bug, Samantha. They come with their own built-in sticky bottoms now.''

Samantha got to her feet, began to pace. "You think...you think Aunt Joan placed the bug under the table?''

"It's just one scenario, sweetheart, but yeah, it's possible. At the same time, she returned your keys, leaving them near the photocopier in the main office.''

"No. I don't get it,'' Samantha said, returning to her chair. "Why would she take my keys?''

"Samantha. If she's the one who brought the first envelope to the office, to have it sent from there, then she knows it didn't arrive at its destination, because whoever was waiting for it told her it hadn't arrived. So she comes back—was she at the office yesterday?''

Samantha considered this. "I don't—wait, yes, she was. Bettyann told me she'd stopped by while I was out. I think I was stalking you at the time, as a matter of fact.''

"Did you take your car, or walk?''

"I walked.'' She rolled her eyes toward the ceiling. "Yes. Yes, I'm sure of that. I walked.''

"So your keys were...?''

"In my desk?'' She shrugged. "I really don't know. But probably in my desk, because I would have used them to open my office, then my desk drawers. Okay, yes, they were on top of my desk not in it.''

"Where anyone had access to them?"

"Well, it isn't as if my office is a high-security area. Although maybe it should be."

"Good thinking."

"All right, so let's go with it. Your keys were there, you weren't there, and someone walked off with them. Agreed?"

"And you think my aunt Joan took them? I know you aren't saying that, but you're thinking it, aren't you?"

Jesse raised one eyebrow as he looked at her.

"I don't believe it, not for a moment." She sighed. "Okay, maybe for a moment. Tell me more."

"All right. If she did take the keys, she took them because she was looking for the envelope that was supposed to have been mailed from here last week. You're the head of the office, Samantha. She knows you oversee everything. So you'd be the logical choice, because Bettyann, or this Rita person, or anyone else, would probably just have mailed the thing. Agreed? She was looking for the envelope, some evidence of it at least."

"And she found it? The envelope, I mean. I don't want to call it evidence."

"No, I don't think she saw it. That's why she came back, with the faked envelopes as red herrings, to see what would happen to them."

"It…it sounds so…I don't know—Tom Clancy?"

"Sure. But now we're doing the hunt for another sort of red October."

"Don't make jokes. This is serious."

"This is also something I can't keep the lid on for very long, Samantha, you do know that, don't you?"

Samantha's stomach knotted. "But you can't! I mean, who would you tell? I didn't bring you in on this because I wanted to break some awful new political scandal. I brought you in on this because... because..."

"Because you wanted me to pat you on the head and tell you everything would be all right. Sorry, sweetheart, that's just not going to happen."

"No, I suppose not. But we can't be sure it was Aunt Joan."

"No. It could be the senator. Which is worse? Oh, wait, I know," he said, shaking his head. "It could be both of them. How's that for a scenario?"

"I won't believe it. Not Uncle Mark. He's honest. And he's really not all that ambitious. I mean, if it weren't for Aunt Joan, I doubt he'd even be thinking about the nomination. He's very happy in the Senate."

"Really? I didn't know that. Ambitious, is she?" Jesse was silent for a few moments.

"What? You have this *look* on your face. What are you thinking?"

"Nothing." Jesse knew it was time to shut up, keep his thoughts to himself. He also knew that Samantha probably wasn't above torturing him with whatever could be handy in the kitchen, to get him to say what he was thinking.

And how could he tell her that? Because what he was thinking was that her dear aunt Joan and uncle Mark were, in fact, planning on selling the presidential nomination to the highest bidder.

Chapter Four

Samantha had walked no more than two feet into the office the next morning when Bettyann came racing out of the coffee room and made a beeline for her.

"Talk. Speak. Utter the words. He is *who?* You met him *where?* He has a brother just my age? A cousin? I'm not hard to please, I'd take a cousin. This would be a good thing, Samantha, because I want to bear his children. My God, Sam, the man is a dream. And those cheekbones? I haven't seen cheekbones like that since…I don't know when. He could slice granite with them, I swear it. Where did you get him? And, if you're going to throw him back, where do I apply for rebound babe?"

"Would you stop?" Samantha said, throwing her purse on the desk and then walking behind it, all but falling into her chair. "Oh, I'm sorry, Bettyann. I've had a bad night."

Bettyann leaned her palms on the desktop. "Define

bad night. Would that be bad as in a you-ate-a-bad-burrito night, or bad as in the man kept me up all night, making mad passionate love to me until dawn, so now I really need some sleep?''

Samantha opened her mouth to deny either scenario—ah, scenario; she was thinking in D.C. talk. How…awful.

"The first one," she said at last, pretending an interest in the stack of national and local daily newspapers that were delivered to the office every day. "Have you checked these yet? Anything for our scrapbook? Anything that might need a press release before the next news cycle? Any mention at all of the senator?''

"Nope, none, and nothing. For the senator, at least. But Mrs. Phillips is on the society page in the local gossip rag. She was a guest at some kind of save-the-endangered-snail-darter fund-raiser, or something like that. Man, the camera loves her. I should look so good, and I must be thirty years younger than she is. Oh, okay, so maybe twenty.''

Samantha hadn't planned to say anything to Betty-ann, at least she hadn't a specific subject in mind, but since the woman had brought up Joan Phillips's name, she decided to do a little judicious poking. "Mrs. Phillips was in here yesterday.''

"Yeah, so?''

"Nothing," Samantha said, busying herself in pretending to look at the headlines above the fold in the many sections of the first newspaper. "That's two days in a row though, isn't it? I mean, I wasn't here, but I think you'd mentioned that she was here two days ago, too.''

"I did? She was? Oh, yeah, she was. She asked if she could make a couple of calls from your office while she was in town, and I said sure, since you weren't in anyway. That was all right, wasn't it?"

"Fine, no problem," Samantha said, her heart pounding. So it was possible. Aunt Joan had been in her office, where her keys had lain in plain sight. The evidence was mounting, even as Samantha's spirits plummeted, because she knew she had to tell Jesse.

"Good. Because we've got to really get to work on this thousand-dollar-a-plate deal for next week, you know. I'm still trying to figure out how we can serve chicken for that amount of money and still sleep nights. I mean, at the least, we should give them the plate to take home with them."

"Funny," Samantha said, rolling her eyes. Then she frowned. "You know, I sort of like that idea, Bettyann. Not for next week, because we wouldn't have enough lead time, but for other dinners."

"You're going to give them their dirty plates to take home? Gee, that's brilliant—not. Although the dish-washers at the hotel would probably give you a rousing cheer."

"No, no. I mean we could give each contributor a plate. A really nice one, dessert-plate size probably, with the state seal on it, the senator's name, the date of the dinner, that sort of thing. And a small stand to display the plate. What do you think?"

"I think you were telling the truth, and you really did have a bad burrito last night."

"Not funny. Okay, on to other things. Do you have the seating chart handy?"

"Right here," Bettyann said, pointing to her head. "I swear I've got the whole darn thing committed to memory after doing it so many times, in so many ways. Do it with the president there, do it without the president there. Do it with the president and the first lady there, do it with the first lady and not the—"

"I've got it, Bettyann, I've got it. You know the seating plan. Now tell me, where am I sitting? Did you leave a spot next to me for a guest, or am I to spend the whole evening making nice-nice with some heavy donor from North Dakota?"

"A guest? You want to bring a guest? What do we do about the thousand bucks?"

"I donate it?" Samantha shrugged. "Yes, it will be the standard donation. There's no problem with that, is there?"

"If you're bringing Jesse James? And we're all sitting at the same table? Couldn't possibly be a problem with that," Bettyann said, rubbing her hands together. "That hunk-a-hunk-a-burning-love in black tie? Hey, if you're running a little short, maybe I can chip into the kitty, because he'd be worth every penny."

"Are you taking hormones or something?" Samantha asked, laughing. "I mean, are you on estrogen overload?"

"We will not discuss my love life," Bettyann said with mock seriousness, "or the current lack thereof."

"You and Benny are still on the outs?"

"And Benjamin is definitely not a part of any conversation that I'm a part of. Oops, ended that with a preposition, didn't I? Okay, Benjamin is definitely not included in any conversation in which I also partake. Better?"

"Remind me not to let you proof any more press releases," Samantha said, shaking her head. "Now scoot, I've got work to do."

"So do I, so do I."

Samantha looked up. "What are you working on? Yes, yes, ending with a preposition. Whatever you've got, Bettyann, it must be contagious. So?"

"A couple of things. Updating and correlating mailing lists for Florida, for one. I wouldn't want to live there, sun or no sun. People keep dying there."

Samantha grinned. It was good to grin, after the long, sleepless night she'd had once Jesse had left with the envelopes. "People retire there, Bettyann. Sometimes retired people are actually *old,* and they eventually die."

"Oh, okay, that makes sense," Bettyann said, winking. "What else? I have to be busier than that. Oh, yeah, and Mrs. Phillips wants an updated list of corporate contributors."

Samantha's ears perked up as she sat up. "Corporate contributors? Why?"

"Mine is not to reason why, mine is but to print out and fax," Bettyann said, shrugging.

"Okay," Samantha said, trying to sound casual. "And, since Mrs. Phillips wants an updated list, I guess I do, too. Fax hers to her, then give me the printout copy."

"You got it," Bettyann said, heading for the door. Then she stopped, turned. "And you do, you know.

You've really got it. At least Jesse James thinks so, you lucky dog.''

''Oh, close the door and go away, in any order you want to do that,'' Samantha said, sure her cheeks were burning.

Once she was alone, the door closed, Samantha looked at the telephone, willing it to ring. She had Jesse's cell phone number, but she wasn't going to call him. No way. He had to call her.

He had to...

Jesse adjusted the badge clipped to his suit jacket and took a deep breath before knocking on the door-jamb. Bob Forrester always kept his door open. It was the chief of staff's open-door policy, or so the man said whenever he was asked.

Mostly, Jesse thought, it was because the man was in and out of the office a thousand times a day, and had gotten tired of closing the door.

Bob Forrester was an impressive man, in reputation, in intelligence and physically. Over six feet six inches tall, rail thin, and with dark hair and eyes, he was often referred to by the interns as Old Abe, after Abraham Lincoln.

But never within earshot of the man, that was for sure.

''Sir?'' Jesse said a moment later, sort of leaning into the room without actually stepping inside. To do that, he'd wait for an invitation.

''Ah, we quoth the Raven—Nevermore,'' Bob Forrester said, tipping back in his burgundy leather desk chair, referring to Jesse by his longtime code name. ''I was just thinking about asking you to stop by and see me.''

"Really, sir?''

The chief of staff sat forward once more, grabbing at some papers on his large, cluttered desk. "Yes. A new report just came in on security plans for the Phillips fund-raiser next week, as the president has decided to be there, lend his support. Personally, I think it's because he likes the desserts at that place, but who am I to question our commander in chief?''

"Yes, sir.''

The Phillips fund-raiser? Could the president afford to be seen with Senator Phillips? What if all hell broke loose before the dinner, or after it?

No. Jesse sighed. He couldn't let that happen.

Yet, at the same time, he wasn't ready to betray Samantha's confidence, act without knowing all the facts. Careers in Washington could be ruined with a rumor, true or untrue. He had to know more before he acted.

"May I see the report, sir?'' Jesse asked, an idea forming in his head.

"That's what I'd hoped. I know you're vetting national security for us now, but you used to arrange presidential security for events like this, and I value your opinion.''

Forrester picked up a sheaf of different-size papers and handed it to Jesse in one big pile. "Here you go. Ingress route, egress route. From the White House to the restaurant, and back again. From the door to the dais. From the dais to the men's room, you name it. Positioning of Secret Service. On the nearby roofs, behind the usual potted plants. Floor plans, everything.

Go on, Jesse, sit down, read it all while you're here. Let me know what you think.''

Jesse sat. He paged through the very detailed plan and found absolutely no fault with it, then looked across the desk at the chief of staff. "I don't like it.''

Forrester furrowed his brow—his furrowed brow was famous, or infamous, in the West Wing. "You don't like it? What's not to like? I thought this was going to be a peaceful morning around here. Not that I'd recognize one, because I've never had one. Okay, this is why you're here, to give everything to us straight, without political spin—so talk to me. What don't you like, Jesse?''

"Well, sir—'' Jesse said, trying to be earnest, but not too earnest. Liars always tried too hard to be earnest. "It's the timing more than the plan, the fact that the president will be there at all, at this time of the campaign process. The plan itself is good. Very thorough.''

"The timing,'' Forrester repeated, folding his hands together on top of the desk. "Go on. What bothers you about the timing?''

"I'm not very political…''

"Jesse, for crying out loud, no matter what we say or what we even believe, we're *all* political. You can't be in this town and not be political.''

"Yes, sir. Okay, here goes. Senator Phillips is running around collecting money left and right now that he has formally announced.''

"Agreed. So are the three other candidates from our party, and the five from the opposition. So what?''

"So, and I'm speaking hypothetically now, sir, if the

president has already publicly decided to back Senator
Phillips, and something were to come out, come up,
come whatever, then whoever he had to switch to next
would look like just what he was, a second choice."

Forrester's eyes narrowed. "Why do I get the feeling
I'm suddenly talking to the Raven, agent, instead of
just to Jesse Colton, currently—and supposedly be-
nignly—serving at the president's pleasure in the West
Wing? What do you know? What the hell do you
know?"

"Nothing I'm prepared to share at this time, sir, because that would be premature. Senator Phillips seems
to be a good man, a good choice. But there are a few
questions that have come up…"

"Damn it," Forrester bit out. "I hate this town.
What is it? Rumors, right? Drinking? Women?"

You wish, Jesse thought, but said nothing.

"So, Raven," Forrester said, picking up a pencil and
holding it at both ends, "when will you know?"

"Can you give me a week? I mean, the press secretary hasn't announced that the president will be at the
fund-raiser, has she? Nobody's planned any leaks? Nobody knows yet that Senator Phillips is the president's
choice, or that he'll attend this fund-raiser?"

"No. Not yet. We've got a leak planned, but we
haven't given the final okay. It's the World Series,
Jesse. If it goes to seven games, the president doesn't
want to be listening to boring speeches, he wants to be
here, popping popcorn and watching the game. We
could tape it for him, but he says that's just not the
same."

"Played college ball, didn't he, sir?" Jesse said, smiling.

"And some semipro," Forrester said, nodding. "And I don't blame him. You ever go to one of those thousand-dollar-a-plate dealies? I never knew you could put so much bad food in one dining room at one time."

Jesse laughed, then got to his feet, placed the papers back on Forrester's desk. "I'm sorry I can't say more, sir."

"You said plenty, son," the chief of staff said, picking up a memo, his attention already on the next piece of business. "Keep me informed?"

"Yes, sir, I'll do that," Jesse said, turning for the door.

"By informed, Raven, I mean I expect to be the first to know."

"Yes, sir, I knew that. Thank you, sir."

"Wait a minute," Forrester called after him. "You didn't come here because you knew I wanted to see you. You national security types are good, but you're not clairvoyant, at least I haven't been briefed that you are. So? What do you want?"

"Another time, sir. I can see that you're busy."

"Son, I work seven days a week, sometimes sixteen hours a day. My wife insisted I show her a picture ID before she'd let me in the house the other night. If you waited until I wasn't busy, we'd never speak again. Now come here, sit down and spit it out."

"Yes, sir," Jesse said, retaking his seat. "It's personal, sir, but as it might have an impact on the president if we can't put our own spin on it, I thought you should know.''

The pencil snapped in two. ''My day's just getting better and better,'' Forrester said under his breath. ''So it's not women or booze. Even the press is bored with those. It's money, right? That's the new thing, follow the money.''

Jesse nodded. ''That would be it, sir. Money. Although that part of it really probably would never come out. It's the other part…''

''What else is there, if it isn't money?''

''Property, sir.''

''Property? Jewels? Land? What?''

''The Chekagovian embassy, sir. I, we, my family, that is…we recently found out that we own it.'' Jesse took a deep breath as two broken pieces of pencil sailed into the air, and began to explain his words.

''Ten million dollars?'' Forrester said when Jesse finally finished. ''That's a nice piece of change.''

''Yes, sir, we think so, sir. Although we still don't know what we're going to do about it. We're talking about forming some sort of foundation.''

''Nice. Most people would be talking about yachts and fur coats and condos in Switzerland.''

''Not my family, sir,'' Jesse said with a grin, relaxing a little for the first time since he'd entered the room. It felt good to have all of this off his chest, even if the Senator Phillips problem was still boiling on the front burner of his brain.

''I know Joe Colton,'' Forrester said, sitting back in his chair. ''Good man. How'd he take the news that his father was a bigamist, that he and his brother were products of an invalid marriage?''

''He's fine, at least his oldest son, Rand Colton, a lawyer here in the District, assures me he's fine. It was the former senator's brother, Graham, who went a little crazy when he heard the news.''

''How so?''

''He hired some goon to find and destroy any papers that showed that my grandmother and his father had been married. The goon, obviously an independent thinker, went further than that, trying to burn down the town hall to destroy any records. Among other larcenies.'' Jesse grinned. ''But Rand says that Graham is very sorry.''

''I'll bet he is,'' Forrester said with a laugh. ''Joe is so honest he squeaks. He probably tore a couple of strips off his brother's hide for that one. But back to business. Your family owns the Chekagovian embassy, and you work for this president. Certainly nothing illegal about any of that, not that I can see. It's also not the sort of thing that looks good in the papers, son, but you already know that, or you wouldn't be here, telling me about it.''

''Yes, sir, I do. That's why I'm glad I'm also able to tell you that the ambassador and his family are moving out next week, to occupy newer quarters elsewhere in the city.''

''That was a stroke of luck. How long was this estate the embassy?''

''Sixty years, sir. But nobody in our family knew about it until recently. So, it's really not anything the newspapers could do much with, except if it's a slow news day or something like that."

Jesse winced inwardly. There wouldn't be any slow news days in the District for months, if what he suspected about Senator Phillips and his wife were ever to become public knowledge.

"I think you're right," Forrester said, getting to his feet as Jesse watched. It was always interesting to watch the chief of staff slowly unfold his long body. The president was actually only five feet eight inches tall, so Forrester was always careful never to stand directly beside him, as people seemed to like their presidents to be tall, as if mere height lent more credibility to the man.

"Sir?" Jesse said, also rising so he could look the man more levelly in the eye.

"It's not really news. Okay, so it's juicy, the Joe Colton part at least, but I don't see any of this coming out if nobody talks about it. And now, with Ambassador Ritka, his family and the embassy staff moving out…? After next week, it's not only not really news, it's old news."

He put his long arm over Jesse's shoulder as they both walked toward the doorway. It was, Jesse thought, rather like being embraced by a giant California condor. "I'm still glad you told me, Jesse. I appreciate it."

"You're welcome, sir."

"And I'll appreciate it when I have the full report on whatever the hell it is you're watching with Senator Phillips. An *oral* report, Jesse. Nothing on paper. Not yet."

With a final nod, Jesse turned left out of Forrester's

office, while the chief of staff headed straight down the hallway to the press secretary's office, probably to cancel the leak that the president would be at the Phillips fund-raiser.

Jesse decided he wouldn't tell Samantha that piece of news, because she was smart enough to know that he'd probably had something to do with the cancellation.

This was getting dicey. He was falling in love with a woman who was loyal to a man who might be the next big political scandal—while he was the man who brought the senator down.

Not the greatest subject for pillow talk...

Samantha was staring at her telephone again, and gave a small, startled jump in her chair when it finally rang and the light for her private line lit.

"Hello?" she said into the phone, and when her mother's voice came back to her she slumped in her chair and said, "Hiya, Mom. How are you?"

Fifteen minutes later she knew how her mom was, how her dad was, how her sister and brother were, how the housekeeper was doing after her bunion surgery and how the lilac on the west side of the house was looking really pitiful and probably wouldn't make it through the winter.

That was the thing with Samantha's mother. You said "Hello," you said "How are you?" and the woman took it from there. Put a few "Wow, reallys" and a couple of "No kidding, he said thats" in there, and you were home free.

After promising she'd fly home for Thanksgiving—

she'd already promised that, twice, but obviously her mother needed to be really, really sure—Samantha was able to hang up, wondering if Jesse had tried to call her.

She pulled a small notepad onto the center of the desk and scribbled: Note to self—Have call-waiting option installed on private line.

"Here you go," Bettyann said as she walked into the office, holding out a thick printout. "Names and amounts, broken down by alphabet, and again by amount. I can do much more for you, master. I can break it down by dates of contributions, even by type of company."

Samantha looked up at the woman. "You can do that? You can break it down by type of company? Like, for instance, you could give me, oh, say, all the mining companies?"

"Sure, why not. This is the age of the computer, you know. A couple of quick keystrokes, and you'll get all the mining companies, conglomerates that have mining divisions, etcetera, etcetera, etcetera, to quote Yul Brynner in *The King and I.* I love that movie."

"I'd like to see that. The breakdown, I mean. I've seen the movie," Samantha said, tamping down her reaction that, if she'd let it loose, would probably mean she'd be dancing on top of the desk right now. "Let's see, let's try it. Mining companies, all right? And oil and gas. Companies that make rigging and drills and whatever for oil and gas companies. Hydropower. Nuclear power."

"Power, period. What you want is for me to give you a listing that includes everyone in the energy industry who already contributed to the senator's campaign, or that we believe will be coming through for us soon. Have I got that?''

"Yes, that's what I want." And then, because it seemed like a good idea, she also asked for something she didn't really need. "And agriculture. I'd like all of those, too. You know, agribusiness? Suppliers, wholesalers, you name it. Is your computer software up to that?''

Bettyann folded her arms high across her chest and gave a quick, sharp bow of her head. "Before you can blink, master, they are yours."

"Thanks, Bettyann, I appreciate that. And then you can go to lunch."

"You're not coming?"

"Not today, Bettyann, sorry. She's got a date," Jesse said from the doorway. "Don't you, sweetheart?"

Samantha looked to the doorway, to see him lounging there, one shoulder against the doorjamb, his eyes twinkling as he looked at her. Her stomach dropped to her toes.

"Oh, hubba-hubba," Bettyann said, taking her time as she walked past him. "See you around, Jesse James. Oh, and you can rob my bank anytime."

"Sorry about that," Samantha said as he closed the door and walked over to the desk. "She's just full of talk, that's all. She has a boyfriend. Benny. They just aren't speaking right now."

"Lucky Benny," Jesse said with a grin. "Are you ready to go to lunch, darling?"

Was she ready? She'd been waiting for his call, for him to show up, for hours. Hours that seemed like days,

days that stretched into years. But fat chance that she'd
tell him that, or look too eager. "Oh, I don't know.
I'm really pretty busy. Why don't we order in?"

Jesse pointed toward the worktable. "I'd really
rather go out, sweetheart."

Samantha closed her eyes, nodded. "I'll just go get
my coat."

He retrieved it for her, taking the raincoat from the
clothes tree in the corner, then helped her into it. He
rested his hands on her shoulders for a moment when
she made to move away, then leaned forward and
sniffed at her hair. "You smell good."

"Um-hmm," she said, quickly stepping away from
him before she melted into one great big puddle on the
floor.

He was so lovey-dovey here, in the office, where
someone was listening. But had he kissed her good-
night last night?

No, he hadn't. He'd been a perfect gentleman. And
all business, from the moment he'd seen what was inside that first envelope.

So this sweetheart, darling, you smell good stuff was
just for here, where the listening device was stuck under the worktable.

She had to remember that. Jesse was playing at being
her boyfriend because it was a good cover for him.
Nothing more. Because he worked at the pleasure of
the president, and that's why he was here, to protect
that president.

Her heart had to remember that.

Jesse carried Samantha's raincoat over his arm because the sun had found its way to the District and

the air had turned warm once more. Just a beautiful October day.

He suggested that they grab sandwiches and drinks from one of the shops and eat them while sitting on a park bench, and Samantha had agreed, probably knowing that he was deliberately trying to keep their location as isolated from other people as possible so that they could talk more freely.

Real *Secret Squirrel* stuff, straight out of the secret agent handbook or something like that. He hated involving Samantha in all this cloak-and-dagger routine, but it was unavoidable.

They sat down on a green wooden bench, the bag of food between them, and Samantha began doling out the contents. He got the pastrami on rye, and she got the tuna fish on whole wheat. He got the tortilla chips, she got the potato chips. They both got bottles of soda.

She handed him a napkin as she said, "You slept last night, didn't you?"

"Fairly well, yes," he answered, and was rewarded when she made one of those scrunched-up faces that he found increasingly adorable.

"I hate you," she said, then took a bite of her sandwich.

"You didn't sleep well?" he asked, already knowing the answer. Not because she looked tired; she looked wonderful. But because she did look worried, and he'd like to tear Senator Phillips's throat out for worrying her.

He took a bite of pastrami, reminding himself he was a civilized man, not a lion on the prowl. No, not a lion.

A raven. Maybe he'd fly on over to the Capitol building and peck the man's eyes out. Metaphorically, that is, because he was a civilized man.

On a very short leash.

Samantha patted her lips with her paper napkin, her manners as refined as they'd be if she was sitting down to a table loaded with fine china and silver, with a crystal chandelier hanging overhead. "I thought about it all night. What did you do with the envelopes?"

"There wasn't anything incriminating in them, even anything to photocopy except for the envelopes themselves, which I did. Then I sent them out in this morning's mail," he said, then banged her on the back as she choked a little. "But not the fifth one—not the first one, I mean. Jeez, Samantha, I'm sorry. I didn't mean to startle you."

She used the paper napkin now to wipe at her watering eyes. "You could be a little clearer, you know. I almost swallowed my tongue. Why did you send them out?"

"Why?" Jesse wadded the waxed paper into a ball and put it back in the paper bag. "Mrs. Phillips brought those envelopes to you, and you said you'd put them in the mail. She was playing a sort of game yesterday, like maybe a game of tag, to see what would happen. If they didn't get into the mail? Hey, then tag, you're it. You're the reason the first envelope never got into the mail."

"Good point," Samantha said, picking up the second half of her sandwich, then looking at him. "You eat too fast. Don't you know that you're supposed to chew each bite twenty-two times, then swallow?"

"Twenty-two? Not twenty-one, or twenty-three?"

"Nope. According to my mom, the magic number is twenty-two. It aids the digestion, and you don't choke quite so often."

"I didn't choke, and my digestion's fine."

"Lucky you. Just don't tell my mom."

"I'm going to meet her?" Jesse asked, knowing he was teasing her, and liking it. Besides, he wanted an answer. He really wanted an answer.

"Maybe. Mom always likes it when we bring home lost souls for holidays."

"Now I'm a lost soul?"

"Maybe not, but you'll look the part if you don't soon tell me what you're going to do next about that first envelope and everything that's in it."

It was time to be honest, brutally honest, with her. "Samantha, I haven't the faintest damn idea what I'm going to do about it."

"Oh, that's great," she said, wrapping the remainder of her sandwich in the waxed paper and shoving it back into the bag. "That's really just great, isn't it? You do know you hold the next election smack in your two hands, don't you?"

"I wouldn't go that far, sweetheart," he said, shaking his head. "Senator Phillips doesn't have the nomination for his own party sewn up yet, let alone the results of next November's election."

"He's getting the president's endorsement at the fund-raiser next week, Jesse. A two-time president, still with his popularity numbers in the high sixties, entering the last year of his last term—which is pretty darn unheard of? With that endorsement, how could Uncle Mark lose? Unless you break this…this mess.''

''Which I can't do, Samantha. We aren't exactly loaded down with proof.'' He averted his face as he said this because he had the feeling he had the word *tattletale* branded on his forehead. If she ever found out he'd told Old Abe to keep the president away from the fund-raiser, hold back his endorsement, there was going to be a war between he and this woman he was falling for so hard. A big one.

She stood up, began to walk down the path. ''Proof? Facts? Oh, wait, you're a Boy Scout, chock-full of ideals and principles and—no, not a Boy Scout. You're a Pollyanna, and everything's rosy, there's no ending except for a happy ending. Sure, right. And here I thought you lived here, worked here. Since when does proof mean anything around here? Facts? This is a lynch 'em, then listen later town, remember? I never should have called you. Never!''

Jesse took hold of her elbow, hoping to slow her pace. ''But you did call me, Samantha. So if we're talking about Boy Scouts, and Pollyannas, let's not forget Pandora, all right? She opened the box, and there was nothing left to do but try to pick up the pieces. That's what I'm doing, Samantha—what you're helping me do. Pick up the pieces. Sort them out. Then act, because neither one of us may be happy about what we find, but we'll both be damned if we'll be part of some sort of cover-up. Am I right?''

She stopped, then looked at him. ''I still hate you,'' she said, but he knew she didn't mean it.

He stepped a little closer, put his hand under her

chin. "No, you don't. In a town piled high with lies, let's keep this honest, okay, sweetheart? You don't hate me, and I damn well don't hate you."

"Oh, Jesse, I don't know if—"

He didn't want to hear what she might say next, so he implemented his latest "shut her up" ploy and lowered his mouth to hers.

Okay, so it wasn't a ploy. It was a hunger he couldn't fight, didn't want to fight. It was a need that burned deep inside him. To touch her, to taste her, to tell her without words that he was there for her, wanted to be there for her.

Wanted all of that...and so much more.

Chapter Five

Samantha sat across the table from Jesse in a restaurant she hadn't known existed until he walked her into it from the street.

The establishment was small, fairly dark, and there was a heavenly aroma coming from the postage stamp-size kitchen she could see through a pass-through the single waitress used to both order and pick up food.

"I know, less than classy," Jesse said as she spread her napkin in her lap…her paper napkin. "But the spaghetti is the best in town, I promise."

"You only say that because you haven't tried mine. One of my meatballs and you'd spill government secrets in a heartbeat just to have another," she said, keeping the conversation light, the way it had been all afternoon, as they'd slowly made their way through Jesse's favorite museum, sometimes even holding hands. For a while, she'd even forgotten the envelope and its damning contents.

"I'll take that bet," Jesse told her. "Is Saturday night good for you? I'll bring the wine."

"Sounds good, if I'm still talking to you by then. I think I like playing hooky, by the way. Are you sure you can do that when you work in the West Wing?"

He took a sip of water from the glass the waitress had plunked down on the table along with two ragged-looking menus before heading back to the pass-through shelf behind the counter to pick up another order.

"We don't punch in and out, if that's what you mean. Besides, Brenda's covering for me. My secretary," he added, when Samantha looked puzzled.

"Bettyann's covering for me, too. Did Brenda ask a million questions, most of them painfully personal, before she'd agree to cover for you?"

"Not Brenda. She knows not everything I do is the sort of thing you write down on an appointment pad. Man, that sounds all cloak-and-daggerish, doesn't it?"

Samantha leaned her elbows on the table. "I still don't know exactly what you do, you know."

"That makes two of us. I guess I'm sort of a…sort of a floater? I'm there to be objective, brutally honest, and lend my expertise wherever it's needed. The president's idea. He wanted someone other than just the usual lifelong politicians to advise him, most especially on national security. I'm it."

"That sounds so official yet so vague. You're not telling me everything, are you?"

His grin was endearingly boyish. "Nope."

"I didn't think so," Samantha said as she selected a bread stick from the lopsided basket the waitress had slammed onto the table. "I'm sorry, we've been talking, so we haven't looked at the menus yet," she told the woman who was now standing there, pad and pencil at the ready.

"That's okay," Jesse interrupted. "Two plates of Gino's special spaghetti with meat sauce, and two salads with the house dressing, please, Lulu. Just ice water, no wine. That's where we start, at least. Who knows where we'll go from there."

"Straight for the antacids, bucko," the waitress grumbled, then headed for the kitchen area once more.

"That was Lulu, the owner's wife. She's part of the ambience."

"Utterly charming," Samantha said, grinning as she took a bite of bread stick. "Mmm…this is good."

"Everything's good. So tell me, have you enjoyed your afternoon?"

"Translation, have I calmed down enough to talk rationally and unemotionally about the envelope and what it means? I'm not sure."

"Well, she's honest," Jesse said, rolling his eyes. "Okay, here goes. I've got the envelope, I've got the contents, both all locked up in a safe place. I sent the envelopes with the blank pages off in the mail, to divert attention from you. They'll arrive at the post office boxes in four different states right on time."

"You just send them off, and that's that?"

"Not really. I've already got people—very close-mouthed people I can trust—all set to watch the four post offices, to see who picks up each envelope, and learn where those envelopes go after that. By now the four recipients have been told that this is only a test of the delivery system, I'm sure of that, which is why my people will be watching those boxes for another week, after the first delivery, ready to intercept any other mailings. Flash a national security badge these days, and you can get in anywhere, trust me on that one.''

''You're very...efficient.''

''That's what it said on my last merit badge,'' Jesse said with a grin. ''The fifth envelope, if we're lucky, will be chalked up to a problem with the mail. End of suspicion being cast your way. When and if the time comes, we'll find a way to keep your name out of everything.''

''I'm not worried about me, but thank you anyway for the thought,'' Samantha said, then realized she'd begun shredding her paper napkin.

''Sure, you're worried, you're in a tough spot. Senator Phillips is your dad's good friend, and you've known him and his wife for all of your life. You've got to be worried that you've opened a huge can of worms better left closed, betrayed a confidence and ruined a good friendship.''

''All right, yes, I am worried about that. Dad would be crushed to learn his confidence had been misplaced. But that really isn't the most important thing.''

Jesse sat back and waited as Lulu put huge bowls of salad in front of them.

Samantha admired the mixture of greens and tomatoes, green pepper, radishes, scallions, even sliced black olives. She didn't have to lean forward to sniff the garlic smell that rose from the bowl along with that of oregano and other spices. ''I could make a meal just with this salad.''

Jesse picked up his fork, stabbing a cherry tomato.

"Don't. You have to leave room for everything else. So," he said, taking the conversation back to the previous subject, "what is the important thing?"

Samantha, her fork poised over the bowl, sighed. "You know what's important. The *process*. The sanctity, if you will, of the election process. Our way of government, our way of life, to get a little schmaltzy about the thing. We can't allow a presidential election to be bought. We just can't."

"Oh, good. Now we're superheroes, out to save the world?"

"I'll be Wonder Woman," Samantha said, trying to keep the conversation from sounding too much like a sermon on good government. "She had great hair."

"Okay then, you'll be Wonder Woman and I'll stay the Boy Scout. But seriously, Samantha, do you really see this as you and me against the corruption of a presidential election? That's pretty heavy, sweetheart."

"I know. But what else would you call it? If Uncle—if Senator Phillips is soliciting money from corporations, a whole industry, by showing that he'd favor them taxwise if he's elected, then he's not only taking money to buy an election, he's also selling himself to those corporations. They'd own him for his entire term in office."

Jesse sat back, looked at her. "You've quite a way with words, don't you? And it all starts with lousy glue on one envelope and a woman trying to go cheap on postage by mailing it from the campaign office. You do know that's usually all it takes—one stupid mistake and an accidental discovery? And then the walls come tumbling down."

Samantha chewed and swallowed another mouthful of salad. "A piece of adhesive tape over the lock on a door, keeping it open, and a curious security guard—like that?"

"Just like that. The mistake, the cover-up, the inevitable investigation, and the next thing you know, an entire presidency comes tumbling down. And it all started with a piece of adhesive tape. That, and a stupid idea."

"This is a stupid idea, isn't it?" Samantha asked, already knowing the answer. "Oh, I mean it could work, but it's still a stupid idea. Stupid because Uncle Mark is already pretty much assured of getting the president's endorsement. Then the party will quietly endorse him, and he'll coast through the primaries, have all the money he needs for the general election. I mean, the presidency already is pretty much his to lose. Why would he do this? It doesn't make sense."

Lulu cleared away the salad plates and replaced them with even larger bowls of spaghetti crowned with a generous serving of meat sauce.

"Some people can't believe in a sure thing, I guess," Jesse said, shrugging. "Hey, you can twirl?"

"Of course I can," Samantha said, neatly selecting another few strands of spaghetti noodles with her fork, then using the round spoon to brace the fork tips against as she neatly twirled everything into a neat little package. "I'm Wonder Woman, remember?"

"And I'm impressed. First time I came in here? I started cutting up the spaghetti, the way I did at home in Oklahoma, and Lulu grabbed the knife out of my hand and taught me how to do it right."

"She is a commanding sort of woman," Samantha agreed, looking at Lulu as the waitress tucked a napkin into the collar of a rather corpulent gentleman sitting across the room. And the man was smiling.

"She could probably lead troops into battle," Jesse said with a grin. "Okay, back to the subject. You want to know what I'm going to do with the envelope and its contents."

"Part of me does. Another part of me wants you to put it all through a paper shredder and forget you ever saw it."

"I can't do that, sweetheart. The wheels are already turning."

"I know, I know," Samantha said, losing her appetite. "And you know what *I* have to do, don't you?"

He shook his head. "No. What do you have to do?"

"Talk to Uncle Mark." She closed her eyes for a moment, trying to picture that interview, and her stomach did a little flip. "I have to take that envelope to him tomorrow, no later, and show him what I found, and ask him if he knows anything about it."

"You can't do that," Jesse said, putting down his own fork and spoon. "Sorry."

"What do you mean, I can't do that? Jesse, I *have* to do that."

"Other than the fact that I'm doing my best to keep your name out of it, the envelope and its contents are evidence now, sweetheart. I can't let you have them back."

Samantha felt her eyes growing wide…and probably wild. "You never said that when you had me give it to you last night. If I'd known that, I never would have—"

"Exactly. Sorry, I don't always play fair."

Samantha got to her feet. "Neither do I," she said, just before she dumped the remainder of her spaghetti and meat sauce into his lap, then followed it with his own serving before she stomped out of the restaurant.

Jesse rang the bell, then waited for the door to open, fully prepared to sacrifice his foot to keep that door open when Samantha tried to slam it in his face.

But it was Rose who opened the door. "Ah, dead man ringing," she said, grinning. "I was told to say that Samantha's not at home if you showed up. So, you've screwed up, then shown up. Sorry, she's not home."

"The security system in this place was one I cut my teeth on, not to mention that I've memorized the code. Close that door, Rose, and I'm in there anyway in five minutes, and that's stretching it."

"You're being a bully," Rose said, wagging a finger at him. "Shame on you."

"Rose, she spilled two plates of spaghetti in my lap an hour ago. Bully does not even begin to describe what I can be. Now, are you going to let me in, or am I going to let myself in? I'm game either way."

"Spaghetti? Two plates? Meat or marinara sauce?"

"Meat."

"Oh, wow. I'll bet you had a fun ride home."

"First I had a fun twenty-minute walk to my car, then I had a fun ride home. And that was only after Lulu, the waitress, tried to wipe me down with a dishrag. Did you know that *lap* becomes *crotch* when you stand up?''

By this point, Rose was leaning against the door, choking with laughter. ''You…you had a real *Lulu* of a time, didn't you? Oh, come on, come in. Please understand that I'll have to tell her you put a gun to my head.''

''Tell her anything you want. Just make sure she's downstairs—unarmed—and ready to go to her office with me in five minutes.''

''Masterful, aren't you? I like that. Excuse me while I drool.''

''Would you just go get her, please?'' Jesse said, but he laughed.

He stood in the small foyer, cooling his heels, and listened as he heard voices coming from upstairs. He couldn't understand the words, but he recognized the tone.

He damn sure recognized the slamming of a door.

''Okay, that tears it,'' he said out loud, heading for the stairs.

Rose was on her way down. She stopped on the fifth step from the top and spread her arms, blocking his progress. ''No, wait, you can't go up there. I mean, sure, she said no, but you still can't go up there. She's—''

''Out of my way, Rose. Please.''

''Gun to my head again?''

''If that works for you.''

''We'll pretend it does. Go ahead. It's not my funeral, but you might want to tell me which tie you want the undertaker to put on you for the services. Excuse me now, I want to go find my camera.''

"Your…oh, the hell with it.''

Jesse took the remaining stairs of the narrow, steep flight two at a time, then hesitated for only a moment before turning to his left at the top of the landing, heading for the one closed door in the hallway.

It was locked. He'd expected it to be locked.

One credit card and thirty seconds later, he was inside Samantha's bedroom.

Nice room. All cherry furniture and white eyelet drapes and spread. Even a canopy over the four-poster bed. Dark green walls with big purple cabbage roses climbing all over them. A dressing table loaded with cut-crystal bottles; the uniquely flowery smell of Samantha's perfume dancing lightly in the air. Family photographs everywhere.

But no Samantha.

He opened a door to his right, closed it again when he saw clothing hanging inside on double racks.

That left one more door.

It wasn't locked.

"Samantha?'' he said as he opened the door, walked into a large, old-fashioned bathroom with small black and white tiles on the floor, a freestanding white porcelain sink…and a huge, claw-footed bathtub.

Samantha was in the bathtub, sunk in bubbles up to her chin, her blond hair piled high on her head, her eyes about as wide as they could get.

"You!''

"Me,'' Jesse said quietly, putting a hand to his forehead, sort of shielding his eyes as he turned slightly away from her. "Rose didn't tell me you were—"

"Why should she? A *civilized* person would have taken a no for a no, and gone away. Humor me, Jesse, pretend you're civilized…and *go away.*"

"I can't," he said, lowering his arm. He wondered, just for one mad second, if Rose had found her camera, not that he needed any reminders of this scene. It was already burned into his brain. "We have to go to the office."

"Are you crazy? I wouldn't cross the street with you…you…you double-crosser."

"Ah, there we are," Rose said a split second after a sudden flash lit the room. "Student pays tuition selling photo of senator's campaign manager and White House bigwig to tabloids. Headline? How about Bubbles Cosgrove and Her Wicked West Wing Lover?"

"Get…out!"

"You'd better do what she says, Rose," Jesse told the girl, who was busily snapping more photographs. "Remember, I can help her bury your body where no one will ever find it."

"Yeah, yeah, I'm so scared. Okay, just kidding. I don't have any film in this darn thing anyway. Shall I lay out fresh clothes for you, madam? I am, after all, your servant."

"Jesse, get her out of here, and go with her. These bubbles are beginning to disappear."

He fought the urge to push Rose out, then lock the door, with him still inside the bathroom. But he was a gentleman, and the women in his family would have helped Samantha string him up if he forgot their training, even for a moment.

"I'll be downstairs, Samantha," he said, one hand on the doorknob. "And no kidding, sweetheart. We have to go to your office tonight. Either that, or I do it alone, and I'd really rather not break in when you can let me in."

"Oh, please, go there yourself. Then I can alert the police and have you arrested and sent to some maximum-security prison."

"You wouldn't do that," he said, grinning at her. "Now, come on, get dressed. Oh, and Lulu says to tell you she doesn't want to see you in her restaurant for at least six months. When I left, she was on her hands and knees picking up spaghetti noodles. She was not a happy woman."

"I'll send her an apology tomorrow, and flowers," Samantha said, sinking lower as the cooler air coming in from the bedroom made those bubbles dwindle even more. "But if you're expecting an apology, you can just forget it. You're lucky I didn't pour the spaghetti over your head."

"There is that, I suppose, sweetheart," Jesse said, and left the room.

Samantha unlocked the office door, then stood back and glared at Jesse.

He turned the knob, pushed the door fully open, then motioned for her to precede him, whispering, "Lady conspirators first."

"Darn right I'm a lady," she said, then began to

sweep past him, planning to turn on the lights. "And I'm loyal, and honest, and trustworthy, and—"

He pulled her back out of the office, and halfway down the hall. "Wait a minute. If you're going to be the Boy Scout now, the Superman, I refuse to be Wonder Woman. I think the outfit might pinch. On top of that, I don't want you to talk in there. Not until I've swept the place for bugs. You are to tiptoe, make no noise, okay? Now, if you have anything else to say, sweetheart, say it now."

"Just one thing. Go to hell," she said, brushing off his hand and heading for her own office—on tiptoe, damn him—to open that door as well. But that was it, that was all the help he was going to get from her. She'd already *helped* him into probably destroying her uncle Mark.

She watched as he made his way around the outer office, holding some sort of James Bond-type instrument and turning in circles, watching the needle on a small meter.

He repeated this action in the small lunch room, in the tiny alcove where the photocopier and three fax machines were kept.

Then he moved to her office.

She followed after him, wanting to see what the needle did when he pointed the gadget at the worktable. Sure enough, the needle jumped, and she looked at Jesse just as he turned to look at her.

"Live," he mouthed, then put a finger to his lips just in case she hadn't understood.

Samantha nodded, biting her lips together to keep from talking. She'd had no idea how difficult it was to keep silent when it was so important not to say anything.

Any more? she scribbled on a piece of notepaper, which she handed to him.

Jesse shrugged, and continued turning in slow circles, watching the needle.

And then he did something she most certainly had not expected.

He reached under the table, removed the bug and *stepped on it.*

"Okay, that's done," he said, smiling at her.

"That's it? You *stepped* on it? Why would you do something like that? I thought you'd want to feed false information into the thing now that we know someone is listening—*was* listening. You know, sort of set up a sting operation, or something like that?"

"Read a lot, do you, huh?" Jesse asked, picking up the squashed "bug" and slipping it into his pocket. "See a lot of movies?"

"You mean it's not like that?"

"It could be. Except that we don't have time for a lot of games. I've got a friend who owes me a favor, and he's going to be part of your staff, starting tomorrow morning. Geoff Waters. You hired him."

"I did?"

"Trust me, you did. Geoff will watch your office, make sure nobody comes to check on why the bug isn't working—and report to me if he sees anything and anyone suspicious. I've got someone else who should be outside right now, and he'll be here every night until this is over."

"Another friend who owes you a favor? Like the

men watching the post offices in those four cities where the envelopes will be delivered? Tell me something, how many people owe you favors?''

''A couple.'' Jesse sat down on the edge of the desk and looked at her. ''Okay, Samantha, the bug's gone. We could go home now, except that you're still mad at me, and I don't want you mad at me.''

''I don't want to be mad at you,'' she admitted, sitting down beside him, her hands on either side of her, holding tight on the edge of the desk. ''But you lied to me.''

''By omission, yes.''

''It's still a lie. It still goes in the angel's black book.''

''Or, as my great-grandfather would say, 'It is difficult for the Raven to speak clearly with a forked tongue.'''

Samantha turned her head sharply to look at him. ''You're kidding, right?''

''Nope. Not at all. My great-grandfather—George WhiteBear being his Americanized Comanche name— is one of those grand old men who likes to say obscure things and have us all believe they have some deep meaning.''

''And Raven? What does that mean? Is that you?''

''Yeah, that's me. He's the one who originally gave me the name, and when I needed a code name, I chose Raven for that, too. I'd like to think my great-grandfather picked it because of my black hair, but I'm pretty sure he was thinking more of my nose resembling a beak.''

''You have a wonderful nose,'' Samantha said before she could think, then quickly added, "I mean…there's nothing wrong with your nose."

"It's a throwback, just like my cheeks, and my hair, too, I guess. To my Comanche blood."

"I didn't know. Oh boy, if I tell Bettyann you're part Comanche, she'll go nuts. She's already waxing poetic about your cheekbones."

"Gee, I'm flattered," Jesse said, making a face.

"You said your family owns the Chekagovian embassy. Would that be the Comanche side of your family?"

"It would," Jesse said, shifting his weight on the desktop. "It's a long story."

"Yes, one you were going to tell me, remember? Now seems like a good time."

"I don't know where to begin."

"Try beginning with once upon a time. That's usually a good place."

"Okay," he said with a decisive nod of his head. "Once upon a time there was a lovely young woman named Gloria WhiteBear."

"Her Americanized name, right?"

"Right. I called her Grandmother. Anyway, Gloria and her family lived in Black Arrow, Oklahoma, where there weren't a lot of opportunities for a pretty young woman, especially one whose burning desire in life was to bring home money to help her struggling parents."

"When was this?"

"Just before the war. World War Two. Anyway, she left home, went West, and ended up working in a casino. A gambling palace, if you will. And she fell in love with one of the guests. He was young, like her, came from here in the District, and had plenty of money, not that Gloria cared about that. She was in love, or so she thought at the time. She'd never seen anyone like this man, never experienced the wiles of a sophisticated man bent on getting her into bed, to be frank about the thing.''

"He only wanted to take her to bed?"

"That's my assumption, and my great-grandfather's, but nobody can be sure. Anyway, one thing led to another—and pretty damn quick, or so I'm told—and the two of them got married within two or three days of their first meeting. She woke up the next morning, and he was gone. From there, I'm pretty fuzzy, except that she somehow found out he had to get home here to Washington—to see his fiancée. He could do that now that he'd gotten what he wanted from Gloria, even if it had taken a marriage license to get it.''

"Ouch," Samantha said, wincing. "She must have been heartbroken."

"You could say that. She ran back to Black Arrow, and that would have been the end of it, except that she soon discovered that she was pregnant."

"Oh, dear."

Jesse picked up the paperweight that depicted the Washington Monument and turned it in his hands. "Gloria knew where her husband—if you can call him that any way but legally—was, and went to see him. She felt he should know about his child. That's all, just know about the child. Except that her husband panicked. He was sure she was there to blackmail him.''

"Blackmail? I don't understand."

"It's simple. The husband had married that fiancée,

the daughter of very rich parents. He saw his cushy world ready to come crashing down on him because of what he considered nothing more than a one-night stand with some dumb, innocent Indian girl who should have had the good sense to go away now, leave him alone.''

"You're angry about that. I can hear it in your voice. And I don't blame you."

"Yeah, I guess I am. He told her the marriage wasn't valid—although we all know differently now. When he told Gloria that his wife was also pregnant, he did it to make her understand that he couldn't be a husband to her, and then he realized that telling her only made things worse. Now she could really put the screws to him.''

"I don't think I like this man," Samantha said. "You haven't given him a name."

"No, I haven't, have I? We'll get to that another time. For now, I just want to tell you Gloria's story. She was appalled that her husband had betrayed her, that he had impregnated another woman. All she wanted was to go home to Oklahoma, which she did. She had the marriage license, she knew her child would be legitimate, and she told everyone that her husband had died. My great-grandparents stood behind her one hundred percent. That should have been the end of it. But the man couldn't believe that was the end of it.''

"He followed her?"

"No, not that. What he did was set up a trust for his unborn child, letting Gloria know that the trust would be abolished if she ever told anyone the truth."

"Let me guess. The Chekagovian embassy was part of the trust?"

"Give that lady a cigar," Jesse said, smiling wearily. "Most of the trust was cash, and the rest was the house—the mansion—which was rented out for the past sixty years, all of them to the Chekagovian embassy. And, for all of those sixty years, the trust was managed by very good lawyers who built it all into a damn nice fortune."

"I won't ask how much."

"You don't have to, because I'm going to tell you. It's over ten million dollars. We just found out, and let me tell you, we're still reeling."

"You never knew?"

"No, Gloria never told anyone, and never touched a dime of that money. She raised her boys—the baby turned out to be twins—strictly on the income from the family's feed and grain store, and never told anybody about the trust. I doubt she even believed it existed. She's gone now, so what we know now is all we'll ever know."

He took a deep breath, let it out slowly. "So, that's it. That's how my family came to own the Chekagovian embassy, which is soon to be vacated. I've been charged by the family with looking over the property, deciding what to do with it. I asked my great-grandfather what I should be looking for when I go inspect the property. He said that the mind will know what the heart tells it. I've got to tell you, that wasn't a lot of help."

"No, I suppose not. What else does your great-grandfather say? I'd really like to hear."

Jesse sighed. "Well, let's see. There's so much. Okay. Last time I was home? He's big into hearts and feelings right now. He took me aside just as I was leaving and said in that profound way he has, 'The raven who seeks will find the heart's truth.' How's that?"

Samantha was quiet for a few moments. "I don't know. The heart's truth? That can't be what you seek now. You're seeking now to uncover who is behind leaking information in that envelope you're keeping from me. Your heart has nothing to do with any of that."

"It doesn't?" Jesse asked, putting a finger beneath Samantha's chin, turning her face toward him. "That envelope led me to you, Samantha."

She lowered her eyelids, not wanting him to see what would be so obvious if he could see into her eyes. "That's…that's stretching things, don't you think?"

He leaned in closer. She could smell his aftershave, feel his heat. "I don't know, what do you think?"

She opened her eyes once more, and the intensity of his gaze sent a sharp stab of white-hot lightning straight through her. "This is…this isn't why I'm…I mean, we really should be…"

Thankfully, before she could completely tie her tongue into knots, he lowered his mouth to hers and kissed her.

His arms slid around her as he moved to stand up, take her along with him, and she went, willingly, her arms slipping up to his shoulders. She clasped her hands together behind his neck and held on for dear life.

His lips brushed against hers softly, slanting, withdrawing, touching her lightly once more. He teased her bottom lip with his teeth, slid his tongue over her softness, then finally crushed his mouth against hers, plunged inside her, took what she had no choice but to offer him, no wish but to offer everything to him.

Their bodies were pressed tightly together as she went up on tiptoe, needing to be closer, longing to be closer. She felt his strong fingers skim her sides, moaned low in her throat as his hands cupped her breasts.

Just when she was ready to give him anything, anything at all, everything and more, he put his hands on her arms and slowly moved her away from him.

"We probably should go now," he said, and she envied him his composure, even as she felt the first niggling rise in her temper at the way he could turn her on, then turn himself off with such seeming ease.

"That...that would probably be best," she said, stepping away from him, turning her back to him as she struggled to regulate her breathing.

"I don't want to," he said, and she shivered as he laid a hand on her shoulder, "but my friend outside is going to be stopping by any time now, to check the doorknobs, stuff like that. We left the front door unlocked, remember? I don't know about you, but I don't want to see Billy come crashing in here, his weapon drawn."

"Billy? Oh, another friend who owes you a favor. I forgot. All right," Samantha said, nodding her head, although she still kept her back to him. "We probably should leave."

"Do you want to go home?"

No, she didn't want to go home. Not unless she was going to *his* home, to be with him.

"I think that would be smart," she said, heading toward the main office. "I'm still angry with you for taking me out of the game. That is what you've done, isn't it? Taken me out of the game?"

"You call what just happened a game?"

"No, not this, although you sure can turn it off quickly, can't you," she said, turning to him, cupping a hand on his cheek. "I mean the business with the envelope. Isn't that what you call it—what they call it in books and movies? Being in or out of the game?"

"What's going on is no game, sweetheart, but yes, I've taken you out of it. From here on in, it's my game."

"The Raven's game," Samantha said, then she sighed. "I wish I'd never brought you in on this."

"If you hadn't, we'd never have met, so I can't wish that, Samantha. I really can't."

"Even if you know I'll never be able to forgive you, or myself, if Uncle Mark is destroyed because of what I've started, what you might do next?"

His expression turned dark, almost frightening in how handsome he looked, definitely frightening in how sincere he looked. "Even if you never speak to me again, never see me again, never let what might happen between us happen. My first duty, Samantha, always has been and always will be to my country. I can't turn away, can't let this go, even if I know it means losing you."

"You think the contents of that envelope are that damning? That dangerous?"

"Don't you?"

She bit her lip, nodded. "That's the hell of it, isn't it, Jesse? We both do. Maybe…maybe it would be better if we didn't see each other quite so often for a while. Just for a while? I mean, this has been pretty intense, hasn't it? I…I need time to sort out my feelings, learn what is and is not connected to that horrible envelope and its contents."

He took her hand in his, lifted it to his mouth, kissed her fingertips. "We'll give it the weekend," he agreed. "I still want you to see the house, and I get the key on Monday. It wasn't going to be available until next Friday, but my cousin left a message with Brenda today, to tell me the place is already vacant. In the meantime, I'll stay away."

"I'd…I'd like that," Samantha said, knowing she'd be crying like a baby in a moment, just with the prospect of not seeing Jesse for four days.

Which just proved how much she really needed *not* to see him for the next four days….

Chapter Six

Jesse sat at his desk in the West Wing, holding the house key in both hands, looking at it as if it was the missing piece to some puzzle he was having considerable difficulty putting together.

He'd been to Rand Colton's office earlier, and his newly discovered cousin had some additional information for him. Nothing much, just that Graham Colton, the former senator's brother, was still moaning and groaning and insisting that he meant no harm when he'd sicced some goon named Kenny Randolph on the Oklahoma Coltons.

Sure. Right. He meant no harm. Guys like Graham Colton never mean any harm. To themselves.

Now he was singing every tune he could, to get back in his brother's good graces, to get off with a fine and a suspended sentence in the "small matters" of arson, breaking and entering, aiding and abetting, conspiracy before the fact—just to name a few of the man's "small" indiscretions.

What a guy. And Jesse was related to him? Gee, that was comforting.

At the same time, he now knew he and his family were related to Joe Colton, that same former senator, and one hell of a good man.

Did it balance out? Jesse thought it had to. After all, was there any choice? Pick your friends, sure, but you can't pick your relatives.

Not that he'd had much time to think about the California branch of the Colton family, or their wealth and many enterprises. They'd all been invited to Prosperino, to the Colton family ranch, and they'd probably all go at some point.

For now, their only connection was one dead son of a bitch grandfather Jesse couldn't punch in the mouth for what he'd done to Gloria WhiteBear all those years ago, and the firm conviction that what they'd learned was private, and definitely not for public consumption.

His family could handle keeping things quiet at that end, in Black Arrow, especially if this Kenny guy could be found soon, handed a deal of his own if he'd plea to lesser charges and keep the Colton name out of everything. Rand seemed pretty confident he and their mutual cousin, Bram—sheriff of Black Arrow—could handle everything.

If they couldn't, then the Raven could pay Kenny a little visit in the Black Arrow jail. He knew he could be very…convincing.

"Except when it comes to Samantha," he said out loud, then sighed.

How did he convince her that he was only doing his duty? That she had only been doing hers? It sounded so…hackneyed, he guessed. "I was only doing my duty." Sure, that's what they all said. Just like the Graham Coltons of this world said, "I didn't mean any harm."

But this *was* different, damn it. This wasn't protecting a family from some old scandal. This was preventing a corrupt candidate from assuming the loftiest office in this land, becoming the corrupt leader of the free world for the next four years, maybe eight.

That was heavy…stuff.

Jesse put down the key and sat back in his chair. He wondered how Samantha had been over the weekend, and was human enough to hope she'd missed him even half as much as he'd missed her.

That was a real kick in the head, too. He'd never been serious about anyone before, and never really thought he was the romantic sort, the kind who could fall like a ton of bricks for a warm smile, a pretty face.

Although it was the spaghetti in the lap that had sealed it for him. God, the woman had spirit. Loyal, yet independent, a class act, and yet with a temper that was all her own. He was crazy about her.

Or maybe just crazy. There was always that.

He leaned forward, picked up the phone, punched in the numbers to Samantha's private line. He might as well get this over with, then go jump off the White House roof if she asked "Jesse *who?*"

"Samantha?" he said after her brief, rather distracted hello.

"Jesse," she said, actually recognizing his voice.

That was good. Wasn't that good? He thought it was good. After all, it had been four days.

"I've got the key," he said, picking it up just as if she could see through the phone lines. "I thought…is one o'clock good for you?"

"I can meet you then, yes," Samantha said, then lowered her voice. "Anything new?"

"Just my blue slacks. Seems my former best pair somehow got tossed in the trash after a fatal meat-sauce accident."

"Oh. Sorry. One o'clock?"

"I'll bring lunch, and we can have a picnic in those gardens you told me about."

"Jesse, it's raining."

"Details, details. I'm still bringing lunch. Tuna fish okay?"

"Tuna fish is fine. Look, I've got to go. It's a madhouse around here this morning. What? Jesse, excuse me a sec."

Jesse pressed the receiver closer to his ear, but couldn't make out more than a few words, although he thought he heard his friend's name.

"Okay, I'm back. Sorry about that. Geoff was just telling me that he got the copier unjammed. He's wonderful. I may not give him back, you know."

"I don't think the campaign could afford his salary," Jesse said, smiling.

"Probably not. Uh-oh, here comes Bettyann, and she looks loaded for bear. She still thinks I brought Geoff in to replace her. Bye. Gotta go."

"Bye," Jesse said to the dial tone, then held the

receiver a few moments longer, as if trying to maintain contact.

God, he was in trouble, and falling fast.

"You free?"

Jesse looked toward the door, put down the phone and quite automatically stood up as Bob Forrester walked into the office.

"Yes, sir. I was…I was going to stop by this morning, but I was called away."

"No big deal, my legs still work," Old Abe said. He closed the door, then walked over to the desk, lowering his long, lanky frame into a chair made for a smaller man. "God, these miserable government-issue chairs had to have been made for the average-size man in 1780. Bought my own, you know, when we moved in here. It was either that or work at my desk all day with my knees jammed up under my chin. Sit, sit. And then talk to me."

"I really have very little to report, sir," Jesse said. Which was true. The only thing he could report, for certain, was that one Samantha Cosgrove had come to him with incriminating evidence that, by rights, he should have shown to Forrester last week.

"Then let me help you, son," the chief of staff said, shifting in his chair. "Joan Phillips is a pain in our collective butts, right?"

"Excuse me, sir?" Jesse worked hard to keep his expression neutral.

"Oh, come on, hark the Raven, don't play dumb. Mark Phillips is such a straight arrow I'm surprised there aren't feathers sticking out of his—well, never mind. He's a good man. Not an inspired man, I'll grant you, not a walking-talking genius like our current fearless leader, but a good one. After eight years of our current commander in chief, he'll be four to eight years of status quo, which ain't a bad thing, because we'll be leaving quite a legacy. He won't rock the boat we built, understand?''

"Yes, sir, I do," Jesse said, waiting for the other shoe to drop. The other shoe being Joan Phillips.

"Now, his wife? There's a different kettle of mackerel. She's ambitious. Damn ambitious, and she doesn't want anyone else telling her husband how to run, how to win, how to govern. She sees strings attached to an endorsement from our president, and she's right, there would be. So she keeps pushing us all away, making her own plans. Oh, she's not above using us, she just doesn't want us to use her. President Joan, I think that's how she sees it."

"Interesting, sir. I didn't know any of that." Interesting, hell! *Damning,* was more the word, knowing what Jesse knew.

"I don't like the woman, that's no secret. I applaud ambition, be it in a man or a woman, so that's not it, I'm not some closet misogynist. It's her tactics I don't like. She's got a lot of bodies hidden, you know. People she stepped on to get her husband where he is today. And Phillips? I don't know. The man must wear blinders where his wife is concerned."

Jesse said nothing, but just kept his own counsel. At times like this, silence was always safest. Besides, the longer he remained silent, the more Old Abe would talk. He knew that from experience, working with anybody he was trying to get information from, bad guy or good guy.

Forrester sighed, then continued: "But hey, bottom line? Phillips is a good man. The man we want. We're all set to endorse him, show up at the fund-raiser, give him our blessing—and then you come waltzing in, tell me to back off a while. I had to ask myself—why? What does the Raven know that I don't know?"

"Probably not much," Jesse said, suppressing a smile. "You seem to already know most of it. You've had me followed, haven't you? I must be getting lazy, because I never thought of that, or picked up on the tail. Shame on both of us."

"Smart-ass. And, yes, I did have you followed. I've even got pictures. The girl? Lovely. You in spaghetti sauce? Not so lovely."

"Samantha Cosgrove," Jesse said, sighing. So much for keeping Samantha out of it.

"Yes, that's the name. Pretty name. She's in charge of the local office of the senator's election campaign. Not the top dog, not nationally, but a good worker, and loyal. And then there she is, one minute being cozy with you, so we think, okay, the Raven's got himself a girl, good for him. And then the next minute? Hey, the next minute she's dumping food in your lap. There's also after-hour visits to the office, and a report that you're cashing in favors and having the place watched day and night."

"Man. I'm either getting very sloppy, or you guys are very good."

"A little of both, I'd say. Anyway, I hear about all this, stack it up against you telling me to hold off on endorsing Phillips, and I've got to ask myself—why? What's going on here? Then I figured, no, I've got to ask Jesse. So Jesse—why? What's going on here? In fact the only thing I don't have to ask myself in any of this is *who*. Because it has to be Joan Phillips. She's been trouble for us before, and I'm betting she's being trouble for us now.''

"I've kept this very close to the chest, sir, working with people I can trust, and totally off the record. No leaks. I can assure you of that.''

"Good. And, considering this town usually leaks like an old iron pot shot with buckshot, very encouraging. You trust these men?''

"Men and women, sir, and yes, I do. Let me show you what I've got, what I've done so far, and then I can tell you the rest.''

Jesse went over to his file cabinet, the one with the combination lock on it, and opened the bottom drawer. He lifted out the envelope, sealed in a plastic bag, although it was a little late to hope for fingerprints, and tossed it to the chief of staff.

"Samantha Cosgrove found this by accident in the outgoing mail last week. The envelope had come open. Because she brought in more envelopes just like it later, we're sure Joan Phillips left it in the office, to be mailed. We just didn't know if it came directly from her, or if she was mailing it for the senator. I think you just answered that question, sir.''

Forrester looked at the plastic bag, then at Jesse. "It's all right to touch?''

Jesse nodded. "Not even any saliva for DNA on the address label. It's clean, and useless for any more forensics, as both Ms. Cosgrove and I handled everything pretty extensively, I'm afraid, before we knew what we had. Standard computer printout, almost untraceable unless we had the machine and could make one-on-one comparisons, and even that would be dicey to prove in court.''

"Court?'' Old Abe looked at him. "This goes nowhere near a court, son. It goes nowhere, period. We neutralize Phillips, and whatever is in here means nothing.''

"Neutralize, sir?''

"Oh, sorry. In your previous line of work that means something different than it does in mine. Remove him from any power, that's what we're going to do. If we're not too late. If we are, then we can't stop it, can't sit on it, and it all hits the fan, big time. I don't want to even think about that scenario.''

Jesse waited while Old Abe opened the bag, slipped out the contents. He pressed a button on the intercom and told Brenda to hold all calls, cancel the remainder of his morning meetings. And he waited, while the chief of staff looked at the ten-page memo, page by page.

"Do you know what this is?'' Forrester asked at last, stabbing a finger at the pages.

"Yes, sir, I think I do.''

Forrester let out a low string of down-home cusswords that had even Jesse's ears burning.

"Where did she get this?'' he asked at last, tossing the pages back onto the desk.

"Ms. Cosgrove, sir?''

"No, no, I can pretty much figure out where she got

it. The question is, where did Joan Phillips get it? Answer? From Senator Phillips. Next question. Did he give it to her? My gut answer? No way in hell. She just plain took it.''

Jesse leaned his elbows on the desktop. ''So you're saying Senator Phillips has no idea this is going on? Has no idea what his wife has done?''

''I'm saying I'm hoping like hell that's what it is. But I have to go to the president with this, Jesse, without delay. So, what else have you got for me?''

Jesse filled in the chief of staff on what else he had done. The operatives watching the post offices for the other envelopes. The bug. The operative inside the campaign headquarters, the one who had the night shift outside those offices—although the chief of staff already knew about Geoff and Billy.

''Blank pages? Damn, the woman's crafty, isn't she? Good work, Jesse. I think you've covered Ms. Cosgrove fairly well, have kept her name out of this. I'd like to think we can do the same. With her, and with the senator as well. Even Joan, much as I'd like to feed that interfering woman to the wolves in the press.''

''Yes, sir,'' Jesse said, relieved about Samantha, and damn glad he wasn't Joan Phillips.

''You know, my wife gardens, volunteers at the hospital, plays canasta and runs her own travel agency. She's glad when I succeed, stands behind me, but she'd never interfere, just as I'd never try to tell her how to run her company, or where to plant her roses, for that matter. Why couldn't Joan Phillips be more like her? No, Joan Phillips has to be a big fan of Machiavelli, damn it.''

He stood up, slowly unfolding his body, and grinned at Jesse without mirth. "So, who do you like for the party's nominee for president next spring, now that Senator Phillips is out of the race?"

"He's out of the race, sir?" Jesse asked, also getting to his feet.

"What do you think, son?"

"Yes, sir," Jesse said, nodding his agreement. "I knew that."

"I'll just bet you did. But nobody else will, not yet. Stick around, and keep Ms. Cosgrove handy—and in the dark—until I can set up a meeting for all parties involved. That won't be until those other four envelopes have arrived at their destinations. I want all the ammunition I can get so that the senator's wife can't wiggle out of this one, and so that the senator understands exactly what happened."

"I'm on top of it, sir."

"Good. Now to keep the pretty spaghetti lady in line and in the dark, huh? That won't be a walk in the park, son, I'm sure of that. Good luck, and keep reporting to me. In person. No paper, all right?"

"Yes, sir," Jesse said, sitting down heavily when the chief of staff left the room.

Samantha stood outside the former Chekagovian embassy, glad the rain had stopped. She looked at the huge redbrick mansion with something definitely approaching awe.

So impressive, and yet welcoming. A home, not a house. A mansion, yes, but still a place where it would not be impossible to visualize children running across the lawn, or a baby carriage parked at the front door.

It was one of the few buildings in the area that had any real land around it, although that wasn't much, not by Connecticut standards, where her parents' home was located on five acres of rolling grass and heavy trees.

This was a city house, yet a country house. Three floors of rooms that had seen so much history.

She rubbed her arms because she'd begun to shiver. Because it looked like…home.

"Hello."

Samantha turned around quickly, startled, to see a young woman approaching along the pavement. Blond, quite tall, she had huge blue eyes that dominated her face, and the walk of someone—although young—who knew who she was, and where she was going. Her smile was friendly, almost welcoming.

"Hello," Samantha said in return. "I…I'm waiting for someone."

"Yes, so am I. Jesse Colton?"

Samantha's polite smile faded. What had the man done—set up tours? It's Monday, so this must be Blondes On Tour? "Why, yes, that's right. Jesse Colton."

The other woman nodded. "Then I'm right, and you're Susannah Cosgrove?"

"Samantha, yes," Samantha said, relaxing a little, but not much.

"Oh, I'm sorry. Samantha, of course. I wrote down the name, but then left the note back at the embassy." She put out her right hand. "I'm Eva. Eva Ritka."

Samantha took her hand in hers, shook it. "The former ambassador's wife?"

"His daughter, actually. We moved out in such a rush that I've been discovering things missing as I unpack. Mr. Colton was nice enough to agree that I meet him here, take another look around to see if I can find anything. Although my father swears things are lost in every move, as if goblins carried them off, never to be seen again."

"I agree with your father," Samantha said, laughing. "I lost my entire treasured collection of colored hopscotch chalk in our move to Connecticut, but didn't realize it until a few years later, when I decided to give it to my cousin's daughter. Oh, here comes Jesse now."

She watched as he parked his car—only one back-up, which really annoyed her, because it had taken her three in this town built for a million people and two automobiles.

"Hi," he said a few moments later, walking toward them. "Samantha," he continued, nodding at her rather quickly before turning to Ms. Ritka. "You must be Ms. Ritka. I hope you can find what you're after."

"Oh, so do I," Eva said as the three of them walked to the front door. "There are a few things we can't find, but one is very important. It's a music box that's been in our family for generations. Hand-carved wood, with the Nativity depicted on it. Not exactly a priceless work of art, not in the usual sense, but it's definitely priceless to us. I can't understand how it got left behind."

"Well, then I doubly hope you find it," Jesse said, pushing open the door and punching in the security code, then standing back to let Samantha and Eva enter ahead of him.

"Oh my goodness," Samantha said, stopping just inside the foyer. Her voice echoed in the empty house. "It's just as I imagined—and yet so much more."

"Pretty, isn't it?" Eva said. "The chandeliers? These lovely floors. I slid down that banister, you know. Just once, and was punished by my nanny, but it was fun, and well worth the scolding. Excuse me now, please. I'll just run upstairs and begin checking through the closets and cupboards. There are a thousand of them in this place."

Samantha only nodded, already walking into the expansive living room, blinking back tears at the beauty that unfolded in front of her.

"So solid. So…eternal. This house was built to last, Jesse. Can you see it, can you sense it?"

She turned to look at him, only to see that he was looking at her.

"What?" she asked him, feeling uncomfortable.

"Nothing. You just look…I don't know. You just look *right* in here. I feel like an interloper, like I should be knocking at the back door while kicking the mud off my work boots."

"Oh, no, no," she said, taking his arm. "This house welcomes everyone. How can you say that?"

"Because you've never seen Black Arrow?" he suggested, grinning. "I think we could put half the town in here, and have room left over for the feed and grain store."

"You make it sound as if you came from the back of beyond, Jesse. Your family is in Oklahoma, that's home to them. Washington is different, I grant you, but a home is a home, no matter what it is or where it is. Because it's *people* who make a house a home.''

"People with a whole big bunch of furniture. I think we could set up a bowling lane in that last room," Jesse said, looking around as they walked through the downstairs, their heels clicking on the hardwood floors. "How many rooms are on this floor?"

"About eight, so far," Samantha said, taking his hand. "And we've yet to find the kitchen. I can't wait to see the kitchen."

When they found it, there were two of them. A small, cozy family kitchen, and a much larger industrial one with acres of countertops, a huge eight-burner stove and two deep refrigerators.

"Excuse me while I try to catch my breath. I think I'm in love," Samantha said, opening cabinet doors to find specialized racks for cookie trays, tablecloths, pot lids—everything and anything that could be organized.

When she opened a set of large double doors and saw a huge walk-in pantry with rolling shelves, she said, "Scratch that. I *know* I'm in love."

"You'd cook in here?" Jesse asked her as she reluctantly left the pantry and rejoined him on the ceramic-tile floor of the kitchen.

"Oh, yes. The smaller kitchen, the family kitchen, is lovely but cramped, the way that sort of kitchen was constructed when this house was originally built. I'd make the whole thing into a much larger breakfast room—those windows facing the gardens are perfect—and use this as the real kitchen for the house. It just needs some…oh, I don't know. Some *humanizing*. You know. Pretty curtains, copper-bottom pots hanging over that wonderful stove, strings of garlic and onions and other vegetables hanging with them, a ceramic-pig cookie jar..."

"Pardon me?" Jesse said, laughing.

"What?" Samantha was lost in her dream.

"A ceramic-pig cookie jar? Tell me, where did that one come from?"

"I don't know," Samantha said, blinking in surprise. "I just said it. I don't have one. I don't think I've ever even *seen* one. But it would be perfect in here, trust me."

"Excuse me?"

Samantha and Jesse turned to see Eva Ritka standing in the doorway.

"Any luck?" Jesse asked her.

"Some," Eva said, sighing. "I've found a blouse I was missing, and a crystal candle holder on the top shelf of one of the closets. Some hangers, which I left, if you don't mind. And one of my father's dress shoes. Just one. I can only hope its mate made the trip with the movers."

"But no music box?" Samantha asked her.

"No, no music box," Eva said sadly. But then she brightened. "I probably overlooked it in one of the boxes we've stored in the basement of our new residence. It will probably take me weeks to find it."

"Well, if you don't," Jesse said, "please feel free to call me and we'll look again."

"Thank you so much, and I'll do that," Eva said, smiling. "I'll let myself out. Enjoy your tour, Samantha. But be careful. This is a wonderful house, and you might just fall in love with it.''

"I already have," Samantha answered honestly, "and I haven't even seen all of it yet."

"That can be remedied, you know," Jesse said once Eva had gone. "If we can find our way back to the foyer and stairs, that is."

"We don't have to. I saw a second set, near the study, or at least what I'd call the study. There were enough bookshelves in there to open a branch library. We can go up that way. Come on, let's go exploring."

She took his hand and led him toward the servants' stairs, and within moments they were standing in the wide upstairs hallway.

If the downstairs had Samantha falling in love, the upstairs nearly brought her to tears.

Window seats, deep enough for cushions and books and cups of tea and long winter afternoons, were in every bedroom.

There were nooks and alcoves and curious little turns that led to one architectural marvel after another. Detailed woodwork, magnificent wallpapers from another age, high ceilings, huge windows, magnificent vistas outside those windows. She felt like a kid set loose in a candy store.

"Look," she said, leaning on one broad windowsill that overlooked the gardens. "Chrysanthemums. The garden is drenched in chrysanthemums for the fall. Aren't they gorgeous? Oh, look, and there's a gazebo. I'd forgotten about the gazebo."

"You're enjoying yourself, aren't you?" Jesse asked, coming up behind her, so that when she turned around they were standing so close together she could make just one small move and be in his arms.

"I'm sorry," she said, ready to back away to where it was safer for her heart. But she couldn't. Physically, she was up against the wall. Emotionally, she couldn't move if her life depended on it.

"I've missed you like hell," Jesse said, his voice low and faintly rough.

She lowered her head, unable to look in his eyes because they were so hungry they nearly scared her. "It...it has been a long few days, hasn't it?"

"Rome was built in less," he said, putting his hands on her shoulders. "You look good here, Samantha. Like you belong. I like that."

"Here? Don't be silly. This place is *huge*. I'd rattle around like a marble in a huge bucket."

"We could put down carpets," he said, his hands inching to the sides of her throat, his thumbs beginning to lightly massage the sensitive skin just behind her ears.

"What are you doing?" she asked, wetting her suddenly dry lips with the tip of her tongue. "I mean it, Jesse, what are you doing?"

"I don't have the faintest damn idea, sweetheart. Maybe I'm finally finding my heart's truth," he said, and then he kissed her.

"Rand? I hate to bother you again today. It's Jesse Colton."

"Jesse, hello. You're not bothering me, you're rescuing me. I've about burned my eyes out reading a brief that could keep Rip Van Winkle asleep for another twenty years. Did you go see the house?''

Jesse adjusted the cell phone at his ear as he headed toward the parking garage, stepping around two tourists taking pictures of the White House. "I did, earlier this afternoon. Great place.''

"I didn't think it was a prefab knockoff of a Georgetown mansion," Rand said, and Jesse could hear the amusement in his cousin's voice.

"Yeah, well, what I want from you now, Rand, if you don't mind, is the name of a good appraiser if you've got one. Is that what they call them, appraisers? I've never bought a house, so I'm not sure.''

"A real estate appraiser, yes. But you don't have to do that. I've got the latest appraisal here, thanks to the trust. We had a new appraisal done for you the moment we found out about the house. Hang on a second and I'll find it.''

Jesse made it to his car while waiting for Rand, and had his hand on the door handle when Rand read him the figure, which otherwise might have been enough to knock him off his feet.

"Wow," he said, his hand frozen in place. "It's true what they say about Georgetown, isn't it? Pricey.''

"Are you planning to recommend that the family sells it?'' Rand asked as Jesse opened the car door, slipped into the driver's seat.

"Yes, that's exactly what I'm planning. I mean, we could continue to rent it out for the income, but I think the family wants the assets of the trust to be all in funds so it's easier to handle. This is the only real estate, and it kind of messes up the works, you know?''

"I can probably help you out, then. I mean, all you have to do is put out the word and you'll have buyers lining up. One of my associates can handle the title search—you need one, even if we know it's a clear title—and the closing when the deal is done."

"Thanks, I'll take you up on that," Jesse said, backing out of his space. "The title search and the closing, that is. I already have a buyer."

"You work fast, cousin," Rand said.

"I'm an easy sell," Jesse said, smiling at his own small joke.

"What? Do I understand this correctly? *You're* going to buy the house? But you already own the house."

"*We* own the house, cousin, my whole family owns that house. That's why I wanted the appraisal, to make sure I'd be offering the full market value less only my share, as my parents have already decided each of us kids gets one share, and one vote in what we do with the trust."

"Nice. I like your family, and I've yet to meet most of them."

"Thanks. As for the price? I got really lucky with a few little security gadgets I dreamed up over the years, so I can afford it, although I'll probably have to work until I'm eighty to pay off the mortgage. But that's all right. You see, I need a house. I need this house. I'm getting married."

"No kidding. That's terrific. Your fiancée must be over the moon if she's seen the house."

Jesse pulled to the exit of the parking garage and stepped on the brake, not wanting to pull out into traffic while still on the cell phone. "Definitely crazy about it. Now to get her to be crazy about me."

"Excuse me? What did you say? Are you saying you haven't asked the woman yet?"

"That would be it in a nutshell, cousin. Probably because she might hate me once I tell her everything I have to tell her. Still, it wouldn't be fair to ask her first and then tell her the bad news. Wish me luck?"

"Sure, even if I don't have the damnedest idea what you're talking about. Keep me informed, okay? Man, I've got to meet all the rest of my new Colton relatives, if you're a sample of them. I think you'll all fit in very well with our branch of the family. Believe me, we're all just a little off center when it comes to romance and marriage."

"We'll have to swap stories one day," Jesse said.

"I'll bring the wine and the crying towel. And good luck to you, cousin."

Jesse thanked him and cut the connection.

He was buying a house. His family would approve, he was sure of that.

Getting Samantha to agree, however, was going to be—as Old Abe might say it—a whole different kettle of mackerel.

Chapter Seven

"No, everything is fine, really. I would have called you otherwise, you know that."

Samantha listened with only half an ear, because Rose was always on the phone. Always, and with everyone. Adding another line just meant that she could talk to more people at the same time.

With call waiting, Samantha figured that Rose often spoke with four different people at the same time, on two different cordless telephones.

Other than Rose's extensive knowledge of Russian history and her ability to grow her nails long enough to stick small decorative decals on them, Samantha most envied Rose her mastery of keeping four different conversations going without breaking a sweat.

"...and then she told him if he didn't agree with her theme statement, he could just blow it out his ear. Can you imagine her saying that? To a *professor?* No wonder she's changed majors three times."

Samantha snuggled deeper into the comfortable couch and smiled as she turned a page in her book, *Political Campaign: Strategies for the New Millennium.*

"...so I told her, I said, Sarah, if you want to wear pink, wear pink, but then, for God's sake, get rid of the orange lipstick..."

"Rose," Samantha called out, leaning her head back on the arm of the couch so that her voice would carry into the dining room, "could you please do me a great big favor and go upstairs to—"

"Yes, I know she shouldn't have dumped the spaghetti in his lap, Mrs. C., but I think she's calmed down now. Come here? You want to come here? Well, I—"

Samantha, who had nearly done a flip as she jack-knifed off the couch, grabbed one of the telephones from Rose's hand. "Mom? Samantha here. Mom, no. You don't have to come here. It was an accident, and he deserved it anyway. And it was only spaghetti. It wasn't as if I'd beaned him with a brick or something. So really, you don't—"

"Wrong phone," Rose said, handing her the other one, the one that had been stuck to her right ear. "You just told my friend Cynthia about the spaghetti caper, which you didn't have to do. She already knows. Trust me, everybody knows. Here—Mrs. C.'s on this one."

"Mom? It's me," Samantha said into the phone while glaring at Rose. "I...I didn't know you had called. Rose didn't tell me."

What followed was a solid twenty minutes of Samantha's mother talking, and Samantha saying the occasional "Uh-huh" or "I know, Mom, really I do," while glaring at Rose, who'd popped popcorn and sat there watching and listening—and grinning like the Cheshire cat.

By the time Samantha could convince her mother that, yes, the bridge tournament to benefit a local summer camp *was* more important than flying to Washington to explain, yet again, that *ladies* do not resort to physical violence, she was exhausted enough to actually thank Rose for putting a bowl of microwaved popcorn in front of her.

"I suppose this is your idea of a peace offering for betraying me to my mother, telling her all my secrets?" she asked her live-in Benedict Arnold. "Um…extra butter. Okay, I forgive you."

"Boy, you're easy. Anyway, you should forgive me," Rose said, curling up on one of the chairs, her own half-eaten bowl of popcorn in her lap. "I talked her out of it, even before you grabbed the phone."

"Oh, really? You're such an innocent do-gooder, Rose, always with my best interests at heart. So? Who do you suppose told her I dumped the spaghetti in Jesse's lap?"

"A little birdie?" Rose suggested, throwing a piece of popcorn in the air, then deftly catching it in her mouth. "So, you saw him again today, right? What's he wearing tonight? Beef Wellington? Moo-goo-guy-whatever? I'm keeping a journal, you understand, and since your life is loads more interesting than mine, I borrow stories once in a while, changing the names to make me look like I have a life at all."

"You're crazy. How you got past the interview with my mother without her figuring that out is still a major marvel to me—and thank God you did, because I really enjoy having you here.''

''Beats talking to the walls, huh? Besides, if I can't get a good job with my Russian history major, I may try doing a little stand-up comedy. Hey, you never know. So, answer the question—how did it go today?''

Samantha leaned her head back and closed her eyes, melting inside with the memories of a perfect afternoon. ''It went…well. Really, really well.''

''Oh, kootchie-mama, I want details. Lots of details. Consider it charity work to a shut-in, since I haven't had a date in three weeks.''

Samantha opened her eyes, sat forward and clasped her hands in her lap. She had to tell somebody or she was going to burst. ''Okay, here's the thing. I think I'm falling in love with him.''

''Hot damn! Talk slowly, I want to commit this all to memory, okay?''

''Nothing *happened,* Rose,'' Samantha said, hoping she wasn't blushing as she told that whopper. ''I mean, okay, he kissed me. I kissed him back. We…kissed some more. And then I had to go back to the office for a meeting with a women's voters group from Indiana, and he had to go back to the West Wing to save the free world. Although, if we hadn't both had appointments…?'' She let the sentence hang.

''What kind of kisser is he? I mean, there's all kinds, a lot of them pretty darn sloppy. Is he sloppy? He doesn't look like he'd be sloppy. So, what kind of kisser is he? Rate him for me.''

Samantha rolled her eyes. ''On a scale of one to ten, you mean?''

"Exactly. On a scale of one to ten."

"Okay." Samantha grinned. She couldn't help herself. "He's a fourteen."

"Oh, wow. Oh, wow oh wow oh wow! A ten. Even a twelve. But a fourteen?"

"Maybe a fifteen. Or a ninety-seven. In a league all his own, Rose. Definitely."

"Oh, stop, you're killing me here. Can I be you in my next life?"

Samantha laughed, but then her smile faded. "I don't know what's going to happen next, Rose. I mean, he seems serious. Heaven knows I'm serious. But…but this is all moving so quickly, except for the four days I didn't see him. Those were the longest, hardest, loneliest days in my life. How do you not know a person exists one day, and then not be able to imagine your life without him the next?"

Rose pulled her glasses off the top of her head, positioned them low on her nose and looked at Samantha through slitted eyelids. "Ze girl, ze iz smitten, *da?* No need iz there for ze crystal ball, ze tea leaves. I zee a wedding gown in ze future. Ze man, dark and handsome. Ze little childrens, all of them laughing, happy, *da?* Ze picket fence—"

"No picket fence," Samantha interrupted. "But there is a gazebo. A white one, with climbing roses on it. They're all done blooming for the year, unfortunately, but I'm pretty sure they'll be red. Red roses look so lovely against white. Although yellow is pretty, too."

Rose shoved her glasses higher on her nose. "You

made up a gazebo? You have been giving this a lot of thought, haven't you, Samantha?''

"I didn't have to make up anything. I saw it. We met today at a house Jesse and his family own in Georgetown. It used to be the Chekagovian embassy."

"Get out! You're kidding me, right? The Chekagovian embassy? That's a mansion."

"It is large," Samantha conceded. "But it's still a home, really. You can just *feel* the welcome when you walk inside the door. It's vacant right now, and Jesse told me the family is going to sell it. Oh, and I met Eva Ritka today, too. She's the youngest daughter of the Chekagovian ambassador. She came by to look for something the movers missed when they packed up all the Ritka belongings."

"What was she like? I've never met an ambassador's daughter."

"She was very nice. Very pretty. I wish she could have found what she was looking for, but Jesse said she could come back anytime, to look again."

"I wish I could see this house. You seem to be fascinated by it."

"I'm more than fascinated." She was quiet for a moment, then shrugged. "Can I swear you to secrecy and really believe you won't go running to tell the world? Oh, and world translates to my mother. Understand?"

"Sure," Rose answered quickly. "I only tell unimportant stuff. You didn't swear me to secrecy about the spaghetti, so I'm guessing this is important?"

"Yes, it is. All right, here goes. Jesse's cousin, Rand Colton, is a lawyer here in town, and he knows all about it. Jesse's related to him, you understand. He told me a lot more about his family this afternoon. I...I phoned him when I got back to the office. Rand, that is.''

Rose sat up straighter, tucking her legs under her. ''Wait a minute. You talked to his cousin—about the house, right? Why?''

Samantha took a deep breath, let it out slowly. ''I...I think I want to buy it...with my trust fund money, and give it to Jesse.''

Rose's mouth dropped open for a few seconds, and she blinked rapidly before saying, in some awe, ''So much for all your mama's teachings. You're going to buy it, give it to him as a gift? Tell me, Samantha, would this be before or after you propose to him?''

''I'm not going to propose to him. I wouldn't... couldn't do that. I mean, if it never goes that far, if I'm wrong, and he doesn't feel the way I do, then I'd just never tell him I bought it, and sell it again. But what if it got sold before he gets around to asking me to marry him? It's *our* house, Rose. I could feel it as we walked through the rooms.''

''As you and Mr. Scores-Ninety-seven-on-the-Kiss-o-meter kissed your way through the rooms, you mean,'' Rose corrected with a grin, then wrinkled her nose in thought. ''But wait a minute here. Won't he know if you buy it? Your name would be on the offer, right?''

''Mr. Colton—Rand—says that can be handled. In fact, he was really quite nice. He asked if I had just been to the house with Jesse, because Jesse had told him about the house, and about someone he'd taken there today."

Then she frowned. "He kept…laughing. I don't know why. He said the house couldn't possibly even come onto the market for another month. But he said he'd help me, keep me informed. We're having lunch next week because he wants to meet me."

"Sure, he'll meet you, feed you, then push you straight into a rubber room," Rose said, sighing. "Lord knows, this is going to sound strange coming from me—the original Miss Impulsive—but aren't you sort of rushing things?"

"Sure, I am. I know that. But did you ever know…I mean, just *know* that something was right? I mean, there are a few problems Jesse and I still have to sort out—something to do with work—but Jesse's special. What I feel for him is special. And I think he feels the same way about me."

"You *think* he feels the same way about you?"

"All right. I *know* he does. The heart…well, not to sound soppy, but the heart just *knows*. Please don't ask me to explain how, because I can't tell you. I don't understand it, I just *know* it."

"Someone should call your mother," Rose said, hunting in the nearly empty bowl for one of the few remaining popped kernels of corn. Then she lifted her head, grinned at Samantha. "But it's not going to be me."

A few days later, after two long, intimate dinners in two more of Jesse's and Samantha's favorite restaurants, after two lunches taken together on park benches…and quite a few kisses…Jesse walked into Samantha's office and sat down, his expression determined, and noncommittal.

He didn't even kiss her hello.

"Your dog just die?" Samantha asked, looking at him across the desktop.

He looked at her. How he loved her. How he hoped she felt the same way…and that their love would be enough to get them through the next couple of days. "That might be easier. We have to talk, Samantha."

She frowned. "You're going to refuse to wear a monkey suit to the fund-raiser Friday night?"

He cracked a small smile. "I'll have you know that I look very good in a monkey suit. Better than very good. Splendid, even. Women faint in my path when I walk past them in a monkey suit."

"Probably when they get a glimpse of the tail," Samantha retorted, balling up a piece of typing paper and tossing it at him.

"Maybe. Or maybe it's the little red hat that gets to them, or the tin cup?"

"Would you please stop," Samantha said, laughing. "Why do they call a tuxedo a monkey suit anyway?"

He knew she was stalling. She had sensed that he had bad news for her, and she was stalling…and he was more than willing to stall along with her.

"Is this going to be a philosophical discussion," he asked her in mock seriousness, "or do you really want to know? Because I can grab Bettyann's computer from her, go online, and probably have an answer for you in ten minutes."

"No, that's all right," Samantha said, leaning back

in her chair. "Okay, I guess I've stalled enough to get my heart rate back down to normal. What's up, Jesse? You said we probably couldn't have lunch together today because you'd be too busy, remember? So why are you here, and why are you looking like a man bearing bad news?"

He reached into the inside pocket of his suit coat and pulled out a typed sheet of paper, folded in half lengthwise. "They've all been delivered."

He watched as Samantha wet her lips, then folded her hands in front of her on the desktop. "The four envelopes?"

"That would be them, yes. The always unfathomable United States Post Office being what it is, naturally we had to wait an extra day for the envelope going to Saint Louis to arrive, although the one for Sacramento, California, showed up yesterday. Go figure."

"And they were all picked up from their post office boxes? Already?"

"The Chicago guy was hanging around the post office waiting for the boxes to be loaded. Everyone knew the envelopes were expected."

Samantha picked up a large paper clip and began unbending it, her eyes on her task and avoiding his. "Your people were there? To photograph everything? To follow the people who picked up the envelopes?"

"Photos, following, the whole nine yards, Samantha. And do you know what we discovered?"

She put down the paper clip. Looked at him levelly. And shocked the hell out of him.

"Yes, I think I do. Saint Louis? That would be PDE, Incorporated, an alternative energy company. Chicago?

Paul Manners and Sons, a large, privately owned company, also energy. They design nuclear power plants, which is not exactly a booming business right now, but could be if the federal government did something about it. Sacramento has to be First Hit Mining, and Butte, Montana, is either Hasbrook Energy or Sullivan Mining and Engineering. So? How'd I do?''

Jesse shook his head slowly as he stared at her. "How? It was Sullivan, by the way, but—how? How did you know? We didn't know, not until we followed the pick-up guy back to each headquarters.''

Samantha unlocked the bottom drawer of her desk and pulled out a green and white printout, then handed it to him.

"Bettyann made up a list for me of all contributors involved in mining and any other energy business, from alternative sources to coal, to gas, to nuclear power. The first pack are those that already contributed, and the second is our list of hopeful contacts for the future. Mrs. Phillips pretty much has the same lists. She asked for them.''

Jesse paged through the printouts, shaking his head. "So, since you knew the cities involved from the address labels, you just went down these sheets picking companies? I thought I said you were out of this, sweetheart.''

"Exactly, Jesse. *You* said I was out of this. I never said so. Oh, and you'll see from the printouts that there are four possibles for the address on the first envelope. That's as far down as I can get it. Sorry.''

"That's okay, I think we can take it from here." He held up the printouts. "May I keep these?''

She shrugged. "I suppose so. I was pretty sure today would be the day you'd get back to me on the envelopes. I've already typed up my resignation, effective immediately, and will take it up to the Hill and hand deliver it to the senator later today in his Senate office. All I need to do now is to put today's date on and print out a fresh copy. Friday night will be my last day, right after the fund-raiser. I might as well go out with a bang. Besides, I bought a new dress for the dinner."

Jesse was surprised. He hadn't expected her to resign. He got up, walked around the desk and helped her to her feet. "Are you sure about this?"

"How can I stay, Jesse? I have to admit that, until you walked into the office a few minutes ago, I was still hoping this was all some grand mistake, even a bad dream. But it isn't. I can't stay here. I can't be a part of this, because it isn't honest, and because I've chosen up sides, and I'm on your side, not Uncle Mark's. That's confidential information I've given you, about corporations on our wish list of contributors at least, even though all actual contributors become public information at some point. So, yes, Jesse, after Friday night, I am out of the game."

He looked at her for several moments, watched her eyes cloud then clear again as her chin went up, her resolve, it would seem, hardened into granite. She was being so damn brave, as all her dreams of serving President Mark Phillips, of serving in the West Wing, went down the circular bowl. He wanted so badly to hold her, to comfort her.

"Let's get out of here, sweetheart," he said, grabbing her raincoat from the clothes tree and taking her hand, leading her to the door.

"My goodness, going out, Samantha? I'd hoped to go over a few things about the fund-raiser on Friday. And who is your young man?"

Jesse felt Samantha's hand tighten warningly in his. He knew that face, that beautiful, well-preserved, smiling face. Mrs. Mark Phillips's face appeared on the pages of his morning newspapers at least twice a week.

He squeezed Samantha's hand reassuringly in return, then let it go, and smiled broadly as he extended his hand to Joan Phillips.

"Ma'am," he said with an exaggerated drawl as she looked at his hand for a moment, then offered hers as well. "I'm Joe Carter. I was in college with Samantha, although three years ahead of her. Prettiest little thing in the freshman class. I just got into town from Alabama a coupla weeks ago and decided to take a chance, look her up. We've been sight seein' ever since. What a pretty little town, this Washington, ma'am. She's going to take me to see the Lincoln Memorial this afternoon. Aren't you, Samantha?"

"I...well, I—yes, I am. Unless you need me for something, Mrs. Phillips?"

Joan was intently looking at Jesse. "Joe Carter, you said? But—but I do believe Bettyann told me your name was Jesse. Jesse James." She rolled her mascaraed eyes. "I should have known. Bettyann is horrible with nicknames. Jesse James was that outlaw, wasn't he?"

"Yes, ma'am. Outlaw or folk hero, depending on who you ask," Jesse said, looking out toward the main office, to see Bettyann standing in the middle of the room watching them. Odd thing about Bettyann—she was always watching, wasn't she? "I'm supposin', ma'am, that you and Samantha have bunches of things to talk about, so I'll just go step outside and give you some privacy."

"Well, thank you, Mr. Carter, and I appreciate it. You're very nice. I won't keep her long, I promise."

"Joe, please," Jesse said, wishing Samantha had been able to suppress that small whimper. He leaned over, kissed her cheek. "I'll be waitin', sweetheart. No rush. Oh, and I'll tell Bettyann what you wanted her to do."

"What I wanted—oh. Oh, yes. Thank you."

Good girl, Jesse thought as he left the smaller office, closing the door behind him. Thankfully, he'd retrieved the page he'd brought to show Samantha, and had rolled up the printouts she'd given to him. The last thing any of them needed now was for Joan Phillips to see either item of evidence lying on Samantha's desktop.

Now to get rid of Bettyann. Samantha had picked up on that one fast enough, bless her. Jesse didn't want the woman and her loose lips anywhere near Joan Phillips, asking questions about "Joe Carter."

"Bettyann?" he said, then coughed, because her name came out in a sort of drawl. It was time to get back to his usual speech patterns. "Samantha asked me to tell you that she really needs you to go up to the Hill right away, up to the senator's office."

Bettyann looked toward the glass-topped door to Samantha's office. "Me? Why?"

"To pick up something that was supposed to have been sent here," Jesse told her, improvising easily. "Something for the fund-raiser dinner."

"Can't...can't I send someone else? Geoff could go. I mean, Mrs. Phillips was going to tell me about her dress for the fund-raiser. Some designer thing."

Jesse gave a little jerk with his head. "Gee, I don't know, Bettyann. Whatever this is, Samantha seems worried about it, and said she definitely wants you to go get it. Oh, and then you can go straight to lunch from there."

Bettyann brightened. "What am I complaining about? With any luck, I can stretch this into a two-hour project, and I do need new panty hose for Friday night. Okay, I'm gone."

"Thank you, Bettyann," Jesse said before he pulled out a desk chair and sat down, his back to Samantha's office and his eyes on the large exterior window that reflected the interior of that same office.

He could see Samantha sitting behind her desk, Mrs. Phillips sitting in the chair on the other side. They were talking. Nothing more, just talking. Samantha seemed composed, collected.

"Hello. May I get you a cup of coffee?"

Jesse looked up to see Geoff Waters smiling at him. "Sounds good," he said to his friend and former co-worker at the National Security Agency, "but I can get it myself. If you'd show me where you keep the pot."

"In the staff lounge. I'll be happy to show you where that is," Geoff said, leading the way then closing the door behind them.

"What's up?"

"Well," Geoff said, leaning his rangy frame against the edge of an old table, "I've got four paper cuts, and I've learned how to put a new roll of black film in a fax machine. I've discovered a pretty good little café around the corner—great grilled-cheese sandwiches— I've talked to at least five hundred people who either want to give money to Phillips or have him burn in hell…and I've found a mole. That's probably the part you want to hear about, right?"

Jesse, who had been in the process of pouring himself a cup of coffee he didn't really want, turned his head to look at his friend and fellow agent. "Who?" he asked, holding out the full coffee cup, hoping he didn't already know the answer to his question.

Geoff took it, took a sip of the hot coffee. "Bettyann," he said then, wincing as the coffee hit his tongue. "She's Mrs. Phillips's eyes and ears in here. Nothing, and I do mean nothing, that goes on in here isn't reported to Joan Phillips. I sure hope you didn't do one of your infamous good ole Alabama boy Southern routines in there, bucko, because Bettyann has probably reported everything but your shoe size to Mrs. Phillips by now. So? Think she made you?"

"Damn it!" Jesse put down the cup he was going to fill for himself and sat down. "Great information, Geoff, but a little late. Oh, yeah, she made me. Which means she made Samantha. She knows now, for sure, who took that first envelope. Damn it! I've got to go get Samantha out of here."

"What about me?" Geoff asked, following him. "Do I stick here?"

Jesse paused, his hand on the doorknob. "Can you give me until Friday night?"

"It goes down then?"

"What goes down then, Geoff?" Jesse asked, looking at his friend.

"Oh, come on," Geoff said. "Mrs. Phillips has eyes and ears, and so do I. Besides, Billy and I talked about it at lunch. Mark Phillips is dirty in some way, isn't he? Him and the missus. And you're going to take them down."

"Go wash your face," Jesse said tightly. "You've got ink on your nose."

"Hey, I was just asking is all, bucko," Geoff said, holding up his hands. "Is she…is she in any danger? Your whistle-blower?"

"No. No danger. But you are, old friend, if you let anything slip."

"Consider me mute, bucko," Geoff said, then rubbed at his nose, just in case there was ink on it.

Jesse opened the door, immediately looking to his left, toward Samantha's office. Joan Phillips was just getting up from her seat, and Samantha rose as well, walking around the desk to give her "aunt" a kiss on the cheek.

How hard had that been for her? Probably pretty damn hard.

Moments later, Joan Phillips walked through the office, calling a cheerful goodbye to "Joe," and then she was gone.

"How'd it go?" Jesse asked Samantha once they, too, were outside the office, heading for the park.

"Fine, actually. She just wanted to know the final

seating chart now that the president is definitely going to be there—the man changes his mind so often I wonder how he can run the country so well. And she questioned my choice of table linens. I told her it was too late to change the color and she said that was fine. And that's it.''

Jesse only nodded. ''You're excited about the president being there, aren't you?''

She goggled at him. ''Are you kidding? I can't *stand* that he's going to be there to put his seal of approval on Uncle Mark. When he finds out what Aunt Joan has done? The president, the whole White House, the whole party, is going to be standing there with egg on its collective face. Can't we stop this?''

''That's up to Bob Forrester,'' Jesse said, taking her hand as they crossed at the corner, entered the small pocket park and headed for ''their'' bench.

''The chief of staff? It has actually gone that far?''

''I'm sorry, sweetheart, but yes, Old Abe knows. I had to tell him. And with the information we got today, the names of the companies…?''

Samantha pressed the heels of her hands against her eyes. ''Do you know yet if Uncle Mark is involved, or just Aunt Joan? I don't want it to be either of them, but most especially not Uncle Mark. I…I've always looked up to him, you know. What happens Friday night, Jesse? Please. Tell me.''

''I can't, sweetheart. I really can't. The only thing I can tell you is that you're out of it, you're safe, and nobody can involve you if this news breaks out, becomes fodder for the press.''

''I don't *care* about that,'' she said, putting her

hands in her lap, squeezing her fingers together. "Oh, I wish there were some...some *graceful* way out of this. Some way that wouldn't be a scandal."

Jesse put a finger beneath her chin, tipped her head up to his. "Do you trust me, Samantha?"

She blinked, then sighed. "Yes. I trust you, Jesse."

"And you'll do anything I say between now and Friday night, and most especially Friday night?"

"I'm not robbing a bank for you," she said, summoning a weak smile. "But, yes, I think so."

"And then, when this is all over, will you let me ask you a question, Samantha? A very important question?"

She took another shaky breath. "You...you could ask it now."

He pulled her into his arms, her head resting against his shoulder. "Sweetheart, I'm going to have to do my duty Friday night. It might work the way Old Abe and I planned it, and it might not. If we screw up, if something goes wrong, you'll always know that I'm the guy who brought Senator Phillips and his wife down, disillusioned your parents, and got your name dragged through the mud."

She sat up, looked at him strangely. "Wait a minute," she said, her voice steady, no longer hesitant or nervous. "Let me see if I've got this straight, okay? You're planning something big for the night of the fund-raiser. If it goes well, you'll ask me an *important* question—a *very* important question—afterward. But if it doesn't, if it all hits the fan—you're not going to ask the question?"

Jesse shifted his eyes right, then left, sort of mentally

hunting through his words to figure out why they sounded so stupid when she repeated them to him. "That had been how I thought about it, yes. But—"

Samantha stood up, glared down at him. "You're such a *jerk,* Jesse Colton. What do you think I am? Some…some *shallow* person? Do you think I wouldn't be able to handle a little trouble?"

"Being a witness at televised congressional hearings, being subpoenaed by a Special Prosecutor, having your entire life put under a microscope by the tabloids, who would just love to make you their latest political pinup gal—that's not my definition of a little trouble, sweetheart."

"Oh. Wait. I get it now. You don't want your name linked with mine if that happens, right?"

Jesse stood up, feeling his own temper rise with him. "That's bull, Samantha, and you know it. I've got my backside hanging right out there with yours, you know. Okay, Old Abe knows now, but he didn't, not in the beginning. I set this thing up on my own, and I probably didn't have the authority to do that. If we hang, we hang together, and that's fine by me—where you stand, I stand beside you, period. But that doesn't mean that you'll like me, now, does it?"

"I don't like you right now," she said, turning her back on him.

Jesse put his arms around her waist, pulled her back against him. "Do you think either of us is making any sense here, sweetheart?" he asked, kissing her hair.

"No," she said quietly. But she didn't fight him, try to get free of his arms. She just leaned the back of her head against his shoulder and sighed.

"So, if I apologize for being an ass, will you understand that I'm on some shaky ground here, and have been ever since we met and I figured out that you were going to be the most important person in my life?"

"Really?" she asked, turning in his arms, sliding her own arms up and around his neck. "I felt the same way. You have a very powerful effect on people, Jesse."

He went forehead to forehead with her, looking deeply into her eyes. "It's all for show, where you're concerned. Inside, I'm sixteen years old, asking for a first date with the prom queen, and scared out of my socks that she'll turn me down. Maybe even laugh at me."

"I wouldn't do that, Jesse," Samantha said, her voice little more than a whisper. "But you're probably right, and you shouldn't ask me that important question until everything else is out of the way, and we can concentrate on both your question and my answer."

"Okay," he said, kissing her, then moving away from her, taking her hand as they walked back toward the street. "But I will tell you one thing now, if that's all right."

"About Friday night?"

"No. About the other afternoon, after I got the go-ahead from my family. I bought the house, Samantha."

When she stopped dead and stared at him, he smiled and repeated, "I bought the house. My cousin Rand called and told me there was another bidder—how anyone found out it was going to be put up for sale baffles me—so I had to move fast."

"Another...another bidder? Imagine that." Samantha started walking again. "And it was your cousin who told you about the other bidder—obviously an anonymous bidder, because you didn't give me a name."

"Yes, you're right. Why?"

"Oh, no reason," Samantha said, smiling at him. "So you bought the house. What are you going to do with it?"

They stopped at the corner, waiting for the traffic to clear so that they could cross the street. "I'll tell you…Friday night."

Chapter Eight

Jesse sat in his office in the West Wing, staring at the telephone.

Did he dare? And, if he did, would his sister be able to keep her mouth shut, not tell their parents until he told them himself?

Sure she could. Sky was a good egg.

His pretty little sister was also one first-rate jewelry designer.

"Okay, for better or worse, here goes," Jesse said out loud, reaching for the phone, punching in the number of his sister's shop in Oklahoma.

"Hi, sis, make any nose rings lately?" he asked when she answered on the third ring.

"Jesse! I didn't expect to hear from you until we all got together at Thanksgiving. What's up?"

"Pretty much, actually, but I don't want to get into that right now. What I need to know from you is—do you have any engagement rings in stock? I know you do mostly custom work, all that turquoise stuff, but I figured maybe you had a couple of regular engagement rings just sort of lying around there somewhere…"

He let the sentence dangle for a few moments, then said, "Sky? You still there? Help me out here, Sky."

"I'm here. I was just hunting up a stool so I could sit down before my knees gave out," his sister answered. "You want a *ring,* Jesse? I mean, I'm on the portable phone, and sometimes it goes a little wonky…but you really said you want an engagement ring?"

"I know, I know, it all sort of comes as a shock to me, too."

"You didn't say anything when you were in Black Arrow, Jesse. When did you meet her? Where? What's her name? Do you love her so much it hurts? Will I like her?"

"You'll be crazy about Samantha."

"Samantha. Nice name. What does she look like? How does she live? What does she wear? Talk to me, Jesse."

"Why do you need to know that?"

"Because I do have some lovely engagement rings here, but I'd have to know something about her to fit the ring to the woman. That's important, Jesse. Does she like modern stuff? Avant-garde? Or traditional? Maybe a simple solitaire? Maybe she's a knuckle-to-knuckle person—you know, wide band, maybe even three rings total?"

"Damn, Sky, I didn't know it would be this hard," Jesse said, sighing.

"Not hard, Jesse. But this is important. She's the one who has to wear it for fifty years, look at it for fifty years. She might not want one from me just because I'm your little sis, the jewelry designer. So tell me."

Jesse leaned back in his chair, closed his eyes. "She's...she's sleek, Sky. By that I mean she's one of those graceful blondes who looks like she should be on the cover of some magazine."

"I'm thinking not *Popular Mechanics,* right?" Sky asked with a laugh.

"No," Jesse agreed, shaking his head. "How do I explain Samantha? Sophisticated yet touchable. Beautiful in a classic sense, but she loves fun, isn't afraid to make faces, look silly. She wears lots of fuzzy sweaters and soft slacks at home, suits to work. Her suits always have skirts, and she has fantastic legs— not that you probably need to know that, but I enjoy them. Oh, and she always wears the same thick gold chain around her neck. Does that help?"

"It helps me know that she likes gold. Would you call her traditional, Jesse? Would that be the word? You know, big soft couches, cherry woods, stays away from the trendy, the latest fads?"

"Yes," Jesse said, sitting forward. "You've got it, Sky. That's Samantha. I bought the house for her, you know."

"What house?"

"The one Grandmother Gloria never told us about, along with everything else. I spoke with Great-Grandfather George and Bram, a few others, and they okayed the deal. I'm paying full market price, less what would be my share. She's crazy about the house, Sky. I figure it's my ace in the hole when I propose, then tell her about the house."

"Tell me about the house, Jesse. If she likes it, I'll be able to tell even more about her. As it is, I've already got my mind down to three possible rings I designed a while ago, in one of my sentimental June-bride phases. I'm such a romantic. Man, I can't believe this. Jesse, getting married. Am I the first to know?"

"Even before Samantha," Jesse told her. "Oh, and before we talk about the house, I need one more favor from you if I can. I have to have the ring by Friday afternoon. Can you ship it that fast?"

"If you're getting married, I can *fly* it there myself. Seriously, Jesse, this is great, just great. And I think it's wonderful that this is all happening so fast, really I do. I don't believe in wasting a day when you've found your happiness. What did Great-Grandfather George say about you the last time I called home? Oh, I remember now. Something about the raven seeking, and finding the heart's truth. Is this Samantha your heart's truth, Raven?"

"Yes, Sky, she is, which means that Great-Grandfather George is going to be spouting even more of his obscure wisdom now that I've proved him right."

"Oh, he already is, Jesse. He wants to call Billy overseas, as a matter of fact, to tell him something about how danger lurks in the big city, and that the night is always darkest before the dawn."

"That sounds like Great-Grandfather George, all right. Poor Billy, he's in for it now, isn't he?" Jesse said with a grin, then told her about the house. His and Samantha's house…

Samantha walked down the stairs, careful to hold the banister because the bottoms of her new shoes were still a bit slippery, then stopped at the bottom to inspect her reflection in the long mirror on the lower landing.

She'd chosen black, although this was far from a dress anyone would pick to wear to a funeral...even if she was going to the death of a candidacy.

Turning slightly to her left, Samantha admired the way the soft, swingy skirt resettled just at the middle of her knees, leaving her legs exposed in almost nude stockings. The scoop neckline, front and back, was almost like an off-the-shoulder cowl neckline, with a large fold-over of black silk that skimmed her breasts, her arms, and all the way across her back. And her waistline didn't look so shabby, either, encircled with a slim self-fabric belt with a small golden buckle.

"Oh, wow," Rose said, walking in from the dining room, licking at a double-decker mint chocolate chip ice cream cone. "Hot mama."

"Thank you," Samantha said, leaning forward slightly as she skimmed a hand over her hair that she'd pulled back in a classic French twist. "Now, tell me the truth, Rose. Do I look professional yet friendly, competent yet approachable, sincere yet—"

"You look fine, Samantha," Rose said, shaking her head. "And since when are you nervous about this stuff, anyway? You could pull off one of these dinners in your sleep."

Samantha took a deep breath, trying to believe Rose. But, then, Rose didn't know what she knew...which wasn't much. All she really knew was that tonight could be a success or a disaster. And that, either way, this was the last night of Mark Phillips's short run for president of the United States.

She went to the hall closet and pulled out her black raincoat, the one that went down nearly to her ankles, and slipped it on. It took her three tries to get her left arm into the sleeve. "Jesse should be here by now."

"I hope he brings a basket with him, because you're going to need one. I mean it, you're a real basket case, Samantha. Here—your purse. You'll need it."

Samantha took the purse from Rose. "Thanks. Oh, there's the bell. He's here. Gotta go."

"I'll keep the home fires burning," Rose called after her as Samantha ran toward the foyer. "Go get 'em, Samantha. Break a leg. 'Ray, team, and all of that! Bye!"

"What's she saying?" Jesse asked as Samantha opened the door, practically barreled into him.

"Who knows," she said, taking a deep breath.

He looked magnificent. Black tuxedo, obviously custom made. Snow-white shirt with small pleats running down the front. Simple yet elegant black onyx studs. A perfectly tied bow tie—no clip-on for the Raven. A soft white wool scarf draped around his neck.

"You look...good," she said, sighing.

"You look like you're wearing a raincoat," he said, kissing her cheek. "Are you going to flash the thousand-dollar-a-plate crowd, or is there a dress under there?"

"Very funny—not."

"Sorry, I was just trying to lighten the mood. Are you okay?"

"No, I'm not okay," she said as he helped her into the passenger seat of his car, then got in on the driver's side. "You've kept me totally in the dark for days,

Jesse, when you know exactly what's going to happen. Did you really think I'd be okay?''

He pulled away from the curb, heading for the Watergate Hotel, the site of the fund-raiser. She'd tried to make a joke about the location at one point, but it had fallen flat, just like her mood every time she thought about what might happen this evening.

"Is the president still going to be there?" she asked. "Can you at least tell me that? I mean, I've got to do some big changes with the seating arrangement if he's not going to be there."

"He'll be there, with the first lady and the chief of staff. In fact, he's probably going to arrive in about twenty minutes."

"No, he can't do that, Jesse. We're only going to the hotel now because I have so much to do, to check on. The dinner doesn't start for another two hours. The president is scheduled to arrive just in time for a small meet-and-greet, then sit down to dinner."

"Well, you know what they say about the best-laid plans of mice and men," Jesse said, reaching over to squeeze her hand. It was only then that she realized that she'd been unclasping and clasping her purse like some madwoman.

"Okay, okay. You're having fun with your big secret plan. Just tell me this—are the president and first lady going to be staying for the dinner? Or are they just showing up to say something terrible to Uncle Mark and then leave again?"

"They'll be at the dinner. I understand the president even has a speech prepared. A few remarks."

"Oh, God," Samantha said, sinking low on the bucket seat. "Please tell me he's not going to take over the night. Our president doesn't know the meaning of *a few remarks*. He'll talk for an hour, while the desserts made up in perfect little American flags of blueberry, pineapple and strawberry sherbet melt all over the kitchen while the staff waits to serve them.''

''Sherbet flags? Your idea?''

She shot him a level stare. ''Do you really think that? *No-o-o*,'' she said with great emphasis on the word. ''They were Aunt Joan's idea. She actually talked a chef into making up slice-and-serve American flags.''

''I didn't think it was your style,'' Jesse said as they pulled up to the valet entrance of the hotel. ''Well, we're here. Promise me something, Samantha. Whatever I say or do, just follow along, all right? No questions, no hesitation, just follow my lead.''

''I'd like to say no to you on that,'' Samantha told him honestly. ''I'd like to say that no, I'm not only going to be standing back and watching Uncle Mark's dreams be ground into dust, but I'm going to help with the grinding. But I can't. I trust you, Jesse. I trust you not to let him be hurt any more than he has to be hurt.''

''If he's unaware of what his wife has done, that's a deal, Samantha. Everybody likes Senator Phillips. But if he's in on it? Then all bets are off, and I have nothing to say about any of it.''

''I understand,'' Samantha said as one of the valets opened her door for her. ''Okay, let's go get this over with before I chicken out and go lock myself in a closet somewhere.''

Samantha had really outdone herself. The ballroom had a lot going for itself, just from an architectural standpoint, but Samantha had used the tables and other furnishings, the chandeliers and dais, to great advantage with some inspired decorating.

No red-white-and-blue crepe-paper bunting, no tacky blowup photographs of the candidate. Nothing that looked like election night in the local fire hall in Black Arrow.

This was class, all class. Silver sparkled, crystal caught the light. Fine china rested on dark navy linen tablecloths. Flowers were everywhere.

"Looks good," he said, not bothering to say more because he doubted Samantha even heard him. She was too busy checking on the flower arrangements, making sure the twenty-five musicians were fed before they took up their instruments, checking the individual table place cards against her master list and the seating chart.

"You know," she said during a break in the controlled mayhem that seemed to rage all around them, "this is a whole lot of work for nothing if this dinner doesn't come off. But you said the president is staying?"

"Five times," Jesse said, then saw the tall, thin form of Bob Forrester out of the corner of his eye. The chief of staff motioned to him, a prearranged signal. "Uh-oh, show time. POTUS is in the building."

"Where?" Samantha swung around, looking for the usual contingent of Secret Service agents, and for some sign of the commander in chief.

"I understand there's a sitting room down the hall. That's where we're going. The senator and his wife are probably already there, at Old Abe's request. Are you ready?"

"Yes. No. Wait, I need Bettyann. She needs to take

over if I'm going to be out of the ballroom." She looked around the room once more. "I don't understand. She should have been here an hour ago."

"Bettyann won't be here, Samantha," Jesse said, knowing he'd just taken the first step toward everything else that would happen tonight. "She's decided to move back to Ohio."

"O-what? She can't—she wouldn't—she *what?*"

Jesse quickly put his hand at Samantha's elbow and began walking her toward one of the exits into the hallway. "Remember how calm and cool you were going to be, sweetheart? Now's the time."

Samantha smiled at one of the waiters, then asked him to make sure the staff knew they were not to serve the fruit cocktail until everyone was seated. "Nobody likes warm fruit cocktail," she told him, then kept walking. "There, how was that? Calm enough for you?"

"Very good. And you're right. Nobody likes warm fruit cocktail. Now, about our friend Bettyann. She worked for Joan Phillips."

"Well, of course she did. We all do. We—wait a minute. *How* did she work for Aunt Joan?"

"Didn't you ever wonder why she asked so many questions, sweetheart?"

Samantha shrugged her elegant bare shoulders. "I thought she was nosy."

"So did I, at first. But, according to Bettyann, she kept Mrs. Phillips informed about everything that was going on at the campaign office. All about you, all about everyone. And she also volunteered, after a few more questions, that she did some private mailings for the lady. Got lists together, printed up computer labels, everything. And then intercepted any mailings that came into the office that were addressed to her directly and had Personal written on the bottom left-hand side of the envelope. Oh, and she planted that bug in your office, Samantha, for her employer.''

"Bettyann? I can't believe this. Did she *know* anything? I mean, did she know what she was doing was wrong?''

"We're pretending she didn't. She swears she didn't. Even as she was delivering those *personal* envelopes to Mrs. Phillips twice a week, unopened, and picking up her extra pay for services rendered. She was going to get teeth braces and a new car with her extra earnings.''

"But, if Bettyann was doing the mailings, why was that envelope there for me to find?''

"The stupid mistake, Samantha. When we pressed her on it, Bettyann remembered that her ex-boyfriend Benny called her to say he wanted to come over, get the rest of his clothing out of her apartment, and she got upset, wanted to intercept him before he got there because he still had a key. She mailed the rest of the envelopes—yes, there were more we're still trying to track down—and left the one with the damaged envelope to deal with the next morning. She figured you saw it, as you were still at the office when she left, and put it in a new envelope, mailed it for her. Stupid mistakes, Samantha. They always happen, sooner or later. And then, as we've said, the walls come tumbling down. All right, here we are.''

They stopped outside heavy wood double doors guarded by two agents in black suits and earpieces, and were asked to show identification.

"You're on the list, Mr. Colton," one of the agents said. "You, too, Ms. Cosgrove." He handed Samantha's purse back to her after inspecting its contents, then reached over and opened the door. He closed it after they passed inside the small room that held the leader of the free world.

"Samantha, hello there. Joan, look who's here, our wonderful campaign organizer. Excuse me a moment, Mr. President," Senator Mark Phillips said, putting down his wineglass as he stood up, held a hand out to his wife. Together, they walked over to kiss her cheek. "Ah, and this must be your young man? Joe, isn't it?"

"Jesse, Senator," Jesse said as they shook hands. Mark Phillips was a handsome man, with a genuine smile and a firm handshake. Not that any of that meant he couldn't also be, as Great-Grandfather George said, crooked as a dog's hind leg. "Jesse Colton. I work in the West Wing."

"Is that so, is that so," the senator said, still energetically pumping Jesse's hand. "Well, Joan, looks like you had that one wrong. Not Joe, Jesse."

Jesse looked at Mrs. Phillips, who had begun to go pale under her expertly applied makeup.

"You're not Joe Carter? Where's your Southern drawl? The West Wing? I don't understand. Were you deliberately making fun of me the other day, young man?"

"No, ma'am," Jesse said, motioning for everyone to go back across the room, retake their seats. "I think you'll understand everything shortly, ma'am, Senator."

"Hello there, Jesse," President Jackson Coates said from his seat beside his wife on a red-and-ivory-striped satin couch. "And you must be Samantha Cosgrove."

The president got to his feet, extended his hand. "I expressly asked Jesse to include you in our little group tonight. It's a distinct pleasure to meet you, young lady."

"Thank you, Mr. President," Samantha said, then stepped back a pace and looked at Jesse.

"We'll sit over here," he told her, taking her hand and leading her to two chairs fitted into a corner of the room, on either side of a square wood and brass table.

Jesse sat down, then looked toward the center of the room, to see Joan Phillips looking at him over her shoulder. Glaring at him over her shoulder. Glaring at Samantha.

The woman knew. She had to know. It was over, all over.

"Mark," the president said, sitting down once more, "I'm afraid I have some bad news for you."

"Mr. President?" the Senator said, immediately looking at his wife. Not hard to tell who was the power behind the throne in that relationship.

Jackson Coates crossed one leg over the other and also looked at Joan Phillips. "Where to begin? Ah, Bob, thank you, yes, that's probably the best place," he said, taking the large manila envelope the chief of staff handed him. One of *the* envelopes. He slid out the contents, the internal memo that had started it all.

"What's that, Mr. President?" the senator asked, and the president handed over the pages. "Why...why this is..." He looked at the president. "I don't understand. This is internal information, even speculation. Committee work. But in the wrong hands—how did you get this, sir?"

The president raised one eloquent eyebrow. He

might not be a tall man, but he was an impressive man, with a presence that made him seem larger than life. "We thought so. You don't know, Mark, do you?"

"Know what, sir? What's going on? Did someone break into my office?"

Jackson Coates cleared his throat, folded his hands in his lap and looked at Mark Phillips's wife. "Joan? Do I tell him, or do you?"

Twenty minutes later, it was over and everyone stood up, even shook hands.

Joan Phillips wiped at her eyes, for she had cried, just a little, before getting herself back under control.

She'd tried to explain away what she'd done, tried to call it nothing more than smart campaigning. She'd even gotten angry when the president told her that special interests would *own* her husband if he got into office.

"Don't be silly, Jackson," she'd said. "Once we were safely in office, they could all go hang. We just need them to *get* there."

The woman was a real piece of work, Jesse decided as he watched them all leave the room.

"So that's it?"

He turned to Samantha. "That's it. Dinner's in ten minutes, sweetheart. Are you hungry?"

"Not really, no. I still can't believe what happened, what I heard, what I saw."

"It's for the best, Samantha. Your uncle Mark is a good man, with a foolish, ambitious wife. But, luckily, bottom line, there's been very little actual harm done. With the senator leaving the race—for health reasons, an ever-popular reason—any money that's already come in can be returned once Mrs. Phillips tells us the details, and nobody has bought anybody's influence or vote.''

''I can't believe Uncle Mark is going to resign from the Senate.''

''It's the only honorable thing to do, Samantha. He and your aunt can go home, take it easy, and she can run for president of the local town council, or something.''

''She could, you know,'' Samantha said, sighing. ''Mom used to wonder why Aunt Joan didn't run for office instead of Uncle Mark. She seemed to enjoy it all more. The campaigning, the celebrity.''

''Don't forget the wheeling and dealing, sweetheart. So it's all over. The senator announces he's dropping out of the race, the president gets to make a very nice speech about the senator's long years of service to his country, and the contributors get to donate their thousand-bucks-a-plate to the party if they want to—and I can't picture any of them asking for the money back, can you?''

''Not when they can say they were the first to hear that Senator Mark Phillips, the top contender, has dropped out of the race, no. I guess I don't have to give Uncle Mark my letter of resignation now, do I? After tonight, the whole office staff is out of a job.''

As they walked back down the long hallway, Jesse heard the orchestra striking up ''Hail to the Chief.''

''We can't go in now, not until the president is done making his entrance, shaking hands with everybody from captains of industry to the waiters.''

''That's all right. I don't really think I want to stay, if you don't mind. I'm certainly not hungry.''

''I know where we could go,'' Jesse said, taking her

hand and heading toward the cloakroom to get her raincoat and his scarf. "It is Friday night, and I do have that question I want to ask you."

She smiled at him, her eyes bright, although still faintly shadowed with pity for her uncle. She stepped closer to him as he put an arm around her shoulders. "I think I'd like to answer that question. No matter how the rest of tonight had gone."

Samantha held her hands clasped together in front of her as they walked into the Georgetown mansion, Jesse leading the way, turning on lights.

The chandelier in the foyer was magnificent at night, and Samantha's eyes began to sting with tears as she looked at the wide, winding staircase and saw, in her mind's eye, laughing children running down those stairs in nightgowns and pajamas, to see what Santa had left for them under the huge Christmas tree in the living room.

"All mine and the bank's," Jesse said, spreading his arms wide as he walked back to her, his broad smile almost sheepish. "Can you imagine what it takes to heat this place in the wintertime?"

"There are plenty of fireplaces," she said as he took her hand and led her through the house. "How good are you at chopping wood?"

"Better than you'd expect. I chopped a lot of wood in my days back in Black Arrow. Come on, I've got something to show you."

"I thought you were going to ask me a question," she said, but kept walking, because he was half pushing her forward.

"I decided you already know what it is, so I did something else."

She shook her head as he took her hands, pulled her into the large kitchen. "Would you stop? You're like a little boy."

"I don't feel like a little boy," he said, taking her in his arms and waltzing her around the large center island of the kitchen. "Little boys don't get to do this," he said, kissing her eyes, her cheeks. "Or this," he said, and stopped dancing, slanted his mouth against hers.

Just when she was melting quite nicely, he put his hands on her shoulders and put some space between them. "Okay. Enough of that for now. I've got a present for you. Look," he said, pointing toward the countertop.

She looked. She saw.

And she burst into tears.

"Jesse! Where...where did you find this?" she asked, stroking the fat ceramic-pig cookie jar. "I can't believe you found this."

"Neither can I. It took three hours on the Internet and a really quick trip to Maryland early this morning, but I've got it. Probably the last surviving ceramic-pig cookie jar in captivity. Do you like it?"

"I love it," Samantha said, wiping at her eyes with a tissue she'd found in the pocket of her raincoat. "I love you," she said, sniffling.

His smile was so sudden, so bright, that she had to press her fingers against her mouth to hold back a sob.

"I love you, Samantha Cosgrove," he told her. "Marry me?"

"Do...do I get to keep the pig if I say no?" she

asked him, because if she didn't say something silly she was going to turn into one big watering pot of happy tears.

"Nope. We're a package deal. Oh, and you haven't looked inside. There's something inside."

"Cookies?" Samantha asked, lifting the lid. She bent over the jar, peeked inside. "No, no cookies. It's empty."

"Look harder," Jesse said, standing close beside her.

And there it was, sitting on the bottom of the jar, in a small ivory velvet case.

"Oh, Jesse," she said, taking out the box but not opening it.

"My sister, Sky, she made it. She designs jewelry back in Oklahoma. She says if you don't like it you can pick out anything else you like better, but she's pretty sure she picked the right one. Go ahead. Open it."

"No, you open it," Samantha said, handing him the box. "I'm afraid I'll drop it."

Jesse did as she asked, removing the ring that, through her tears, she saw only as a mass of rich gold and a sparkle that she could swear lit half the room.

And then he went down on one knee—right there in the kitchen, dressed in his tuxedo—and slipped the ring on her finger. Kissed her hand. "The pig is yours. And the ring. And the house. Will you marry us?"

"Yes. Oh, yes. I'll marry you. I'll marry all of you."

She held out her arms to him, longing for him to stand up, for him to hold her, but he stayed where he was. He raised a finger and said, "One more question."

She knelt down and slid her arms around his neck.

"When? Anytime. Tonight. Tomorrow. Next week. I'll marry you every week if you want."

"No, that's not it," he said, pulling her close. "I have a special request. I want to know if we can serve spaghetti and meat sauce at the reception."

"Oh, Jesse, I love you," Samantha said, and pulled him to her for a kiss.

* * * * *

As a special treat,
the OKLAHOMA COLTONS' *series*
spins off next month
with the single title anthology,
A COLTON FAMILY CHRISTMAS (10/02),
by Judy Christenberry, Linda Turner
and Carolyn Zane.
The spellbinding family saga
returns to Silhouette Romance in November
with Teresa Southwick's
SKY FULL OF PROMISE (RS #1624, 11/02).

Silhouette

SPECIAL EDITION™

&

SILHOUETTE *Romance*®

present a new series about the proud,
passion-driven dynasty

THE COLTONS

**You loved the California Coltons, now discover
the Coltons of Black Arrow, Oklahoma.
Comanche blood courses through their veins,
but a brand-new birthright awaits them....**

WHITE DOVE'S PROMISE by Stella Bagwell (7/02, SE#1478)

THE COYOTE'S CRY by Jackie Merritt (8/02, SE#1484)

WILLOW IN BLOOM by Victoria Pade (9/02, SE#1490)

THE RAVEN'S ASSIGNMENT by Kasey Michaels (9/02, SR#1613)

A COLTON FAMILY CHRISTMAS by Judy Christenberry,
Linda Turner and Carolyn Zane (10/02, Silhouette Single Title)

SKY FULL OF PROMISE by Teresa Southwick (11/02, SR#1624)

THE WOLF'S SURRENDER by Sandra Steffen (12/02, SR#1630)

*Look for these titles
wherever Silhouette books are sold!*

Silhouette®

Where love comes alive™

Visit Silhouette at www.eHarlequin.com   SSECOLT

If you enjoyed what you just read,
then we've got an offer you can't resist!

Take 2 bestselling love stories FREE!

Plus get a FREE surprise gift!

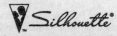

SILHOUETTE *Romance*

COMING NEXT MONTH

#1618 THE WILL TO LOVE—Lindsay McKenna
Morgan's Mercenaries: Ultimate Rescue
With her community destroyed by an earthquake, Deputy Sheriff
Kerry Chelton turned to Sergeant Quinn Grayson to help establish order
and rebuild. But when Kerry was injured, Quinn began to realize that no
devastation compared to losing Kerry....

#1619 THE RANCHER'S PROMISE—Jodi O'Donnell
Bridgewater Bachelors
Lara Dearborn's new boss was none other than Connor Brody—the
son of her sworn enemy! Connor had worked his entire life to escape
Mick Brody's legacy. But could he have a future with Lara when the
truth about their fathers came out?

#1620 FOR THE TAKING—Lilian Darcy
A Tale of the Sea
Thalassa Morgan wanted to put the past behind her, something that Lou-
can—claimant of the Pacifica throne—wouldn't allow. Reluctantly she
returned to Pacifica as his wife to restore order to their kingdom. But
her sexy, uncompromising husband proved to be far more dangerous
than the nightmares haunting her....

#1621 CROWNS AND A CRADLE—Valerie Parv
The Carramer Legacy
She thought she'd won a vacation to Carramer—but discovered her
true identity! Sarah McInnes's grandfather was Prince Henry Valmont—
and her one-year-old son the royal heir! Now, handsome, intense Prince
Josquin had to persuade her to stay—but were his motives political or
personal?

#1622 THE BILLIONAIRE'S BARGAIN—Myrna Mackenzie
The Wedding Auction
What does a confirmed bachelor stuck caring for his eighteen-month-
old twin brothers do? Buy help from a woman auctioning her services
for charity! But beautiful April Pruitt was no ordinary nanny, and
Dylan Valentine wondered if his bachelorhood was the next item on
the block!

#1623 THE SHERIFF'S 6-YEAR-OLD SECRET—Donna Clayton
The Thunder Clan
Nathan Thunder avoided intimate relationships—and discovering he had
an independent six-year-old daughter wasn't going to change that!
Gwen Fleming wanted to help her teenage brother. Could two mis-
matched families find true love?

Visit Silhouette at www.eHarlequin.com   SRCNM0902